HAGRIDDEN

HAGRIDDEN

Samuel Snoek-Brown

Columbus Press
P.O. Box 91028
Columbus, OH 43209
www.ColumbusPressBooks.com

EDITOR
Brad Pauquette

PROOFREADER
Emily Hitchcock

ARTWORK, DESIGN & PRODUCTION
Columbus Publishing Lab
www.ColumbusPublishingLab.com

Hardback ISBN 978-1-63337-990-9
Paperback ISBN 978-0-9891737-9-7
Ebook ISBN 978-1-63337-999-2

Printed in the United States of America
1 3 5 7 9 10 8 6 4 2

"I hate weary days of inaction. Yet what can women do but wait and suffer?"
Kate Stone, Louisiana, June 10, 1861

"We have wept enough; it's time to cut some wood."
Madeleine LeBlanc, Acadian Settler

For Jennifer, my heart and my home.

And for every civilian who ever lived through a war or is living through one now.

I

The women waited, their weapons never far from hand, but for days on end the only sound in the marsh was the wind in the rushes. Those who knew how to discern them might have made out other sounds, the soft splash of a gator slipping from the prairie grass into the muck and water, the rustle of ducks breaking for the sky or the dip of a heron beak as it fished the shallows. But for those luckless strangers who drifted into the saltmarsh, the denizens therein kept quiet enough that by day few sounds were louder than the sighing of the reeds, and at night the baritone croak of the frogs was cheerless and departed. The two women listened anyway, silent and languid themselves in their meager chores, and when at last they'd catch out of the hot breeze the long-off reports of cannonshot or rifle fire, they would set aside their baskets of wash or reel in the crawfish traps, and they would gather their one musket with its fixed bayonet and a long pole they'd sharpened and wrapped with a grip, and they would crawl out into the reed bed to lie in wait.

Such events were rare and getting rarer, but when it happened it would happen the same. A distant skirmish fled of deserters and those who pursued them—sooner or later the fugitive combatants found their way into the marsh, where they hoped to hide. So it was on this occasion, a handful of Confederates chasing a pair of Federals, one wounded and the other beyond his limit. The Federals hobbled under the weight of each other as fast as they could manage and traced a meandering path sometimes on the loamy earth, hidden in the grasses, and sometimes into the murky water, where they joined all manner of other vile fauna. Two Confederate cavalrymen patrolled the rim of the reed beds, stood their mounts for a vantage over the heads of the reeds, but the lone Confederate infantryman, not far from his own homeland, charged unafraid into the reeds to track the Federal escapees. At length they slowed enough to hear above the wind the commands of the cavalry, one Confederate calling out to the other that the pursuit would prove fruitless. Let the damned marsh have the men, shouted one. A splash of hooves and shortly after the muted gallop of the horses charging away, and then the two wounded Federals could hear only their own movement in the reeds, and knew not whether the infantryman still pursued them. Exhausted from running, they limped and shuffled several paces more until they came to a crushed bedding in the reeds. The man worse wounded held fast to the shoulder of his compatriot and weighted him to stop.

Set me down, Charles, set me down.

Charles let his friend gently to the bed of reeds, then collapsed himself. There they lay for long minutes, panting the both of them. A chorus of insects began around them, and the reedheads danced in the hot wind. The two Federals listened but heard nothing.

I think we oughtn't to wait here too long, the bleeding man said. I think you ought to carry on yourself.

Charles waved away the suggestion, turned to face his friend flat beside him and said, Hush now, James, we need to keep quiet and rest a bit.

They breathed hard in the hot afternoon, James bleeding into the earth and Charles rubbing at his shoulder. Then the insects stopped chirring and a cloud of them rose to float away in the patch of sky above them. Charles sat up in the small clearing, the reeds brushing his shoulders. James hauled himself up onto his elbow with a groan but Charles clapped a hand on his shin and shushed him. Something's coming this way, he whispered.

He stood and gripped his friend's uniform lapel and hauled him forth as well, both of them stooped and wavering and then they gasped together, a sound like a loud cough, each man skewered and lifted upright. One on the end of the bayonet and the other on the sharpened pole. They clung to their respective spits in surprise, and then Charles fumbled for his pistol holster and tried to back himself off the bayonet but the antique musket followed him into the small clearing, at the end of it an old woman with the butt against her hip. He paused in disbelief and beheld her as one might behold one's own visage in negative, a dark doppelganger that you understand to mean your end because only one can survive. The woman watched him too but her eyes were narrow and wary. She glanced at James quavering aloft on his pole, a small tent in the back of his uniform seeping black where the sharpened pole protruded through his back. Once she'd seen he was dying fast she returned her gaze to Charles. He blinked and thought to say something, his lips moving without words, then he fumbled again at his holster, but she sneered and twisted the musket so the bayonet ripped open its puncture and he could hear a wheeze of air through the gap in his chest where once a lung had been. He fell against the blade and dropped to his knees and she let him. Then his friend fell over beside him, already dead.

Charles gasped in the loam, his mouth opening and closing like a landed fish. His eyes rolled in his head and he saw the older woman emerge fully from the reeds. She might have been younger than he'd given her credit because he could see now the life that had hardened her face, the flesh weathered premature and the hair streaked with gray like brushed iron but not yet white, her form lithe from hard work. Beside her a young girl only seventeen or so crawled through the reeds as well, her matted hair dark red like dried blood and her eyes narrow and black, her hips boyish. She took hold of the pole by its leather grip and yanked it loose from the dead man beside him. She kicked James's body in the ribs and then pressed the bloody point to his throat as she leaned close to his face. She waved a small hand slowly under his nose, then lifted an eyelid with one finger. The older woman observed all this and waited, then the girl nodded at her and they both turned to Charles.

His breath came raspy in his hollow chest but he dragged in enough air to speak and he said, What are you doing? but he got no reply. The woman held tight to the musket and waited, but to what purpose he couldn't see. She raised her head and listened, then she jerked her head at the girl and the girl slipped backward into the reeds with her bloody pole and disappeared. The woman looked back at Charles and lifted her hand, pressed a finger to her lips. He hauled in another breath and tried to scream around the blade in his chest but he couldn't manage it, only yelped pathetically and coughed a wad of blood up over his chin and one cheek. The woman paid him no attention; she was watching the narrow perimeter of the clearing. After a moment Charles heard it too— a rustle and then the Confederate infantryman emerged from the reeds, his rifle aimed at the woman then at Charles. He studied the scene a moment and then he lowered his rifle and grinned.

This is a fine service you done us, ma'am. He nodded at Charles on the ground. I wish they's more men around to do this sort of thing but you done the South proud as a woman. He leaned and took a grip on her musket barrel and pried the bayonet from Charles's chest; the fallen man cried out, tears and blood hot in his eyes. The woman tightened her grip on the musket stock and yanked it free from the infantryman.

He laughed. Alright now, ma'am, I ain't gonna take it from you. It's just he's worth more's a prisoner, much as I hate to say it. To me anyways. Might get me some leave time, bringing him in.

He smiled at the old woman, then he shouted and lurched to the side and dropped his rifle. The girl stepped forth again from the reeds, the pole tight in her fists and the Confederate on the end of it. She pressed on, pushing the pole deeper into his side until he vomited blood over Charles's chest and then the Confederate fell as well, clutching the pole in his ribs. The girl leaned over him and looked at his face. The Confederate turned to Charles beside him on the ground with eyes wide and pleading, but Charles was floundering his hands over the ground for the dropped rifle. The old woman kicked at it and brought it up with her foot, tossed it aside into the reeds. The Confederate looked back at the girl; she studied him then untied a kerchief from around her hair and draped it carefully over the Confederate's chest. He swiped at it but she pushed his hand away and then knelt on his arm.

He gazed into her eyes. Ma'am, ma'am? He looked again at Charles and back to the girl. Why's y'all doing this? Ma'am? but whatever his last words would have been, they were lost in a gurgle as the girl slit his throat, the blood spraying into the marsh and onto her as well. The blood soaked the kerchief on his chest, and she held it gently away from his coat so as not to stain it further. Charles watched in fascination, understanding at last, and when he looked up again to the woman she had raised the musket to strike again and he decided to look skyward one last time. There a distant cloud hovered over the gap in the reeds, but whether it was a cloud of nature's making or a drifting wisp of cannon smoke he could not tell, and then he was dead.

The two women knelt in the reed bed and set to stripping the bodies. The wounded Federal still wore his scabbard, but none of the men carried their swords. The women laid the pistols and two long knives alongside the Confederate rifle and hauled off the Federal's boots. The Confederate's sorry hand-patched booties they pitched into the marsh. The Confederate wore a small pouch on his belt but it contained only a fistful of hardtack and a plug of tobacco and a clay pipe now broken. They pitched the hardtack into the marsh after his shoes and set aside the other items in their pouch, along with his wooden canteen and his one letter to some love lost. They searched him further but found nothing else, not even spare load for his rifle. One of the Federals wore a haversack and in it they found a mothridden wool blanket and a powder magazine and a change of socks. They found a plug of sticky tar in a tin that smelled like burned coffee and they thought to pitch it away but changed their minds and added the tin to the pile. A sheaf of letters, an eclectic collection of mess dishes, a photograph, the sixth they'd ever seen. They undid the buttons on coats and shirts and trousers with care, then rolled the bodies and shoved them into various postures as they shucked them of their uniforms. The wounded man had pissed himself and in his death the Confederate had shat his drawers but they did not strip the underclothes anyway. When the men were naked save their soiled drawers the women rolled them supine, two men side by side and the third piled crossways atop them, though which man was which they now could not tell nor did they care. They stepped over the parallel men and took a pair of ankles each, and using the two bodies as a sled for the third they dragged them out across the reed beds. They scared a heron skyward as they left.

They took almost half an hour to drag the men to the forgotten well in the marsh, near a long-abandoned homestead where now remained only the well and a packed foundation they alone would recognize. In the gray shadow of tall grasses, a wiry dog watched them. Each woman dragged her corpse to the well and propped the naked ankles atop the stone rim. With such a ramp created, they bent and rolled the third man like a log up the bodies until his rump hung over the lip, and they pushed so he bent in the middle and fell into the well. Echoing up from the maw came a wet crunch of various limbs when he landed in the deep below, the bodies down there already risen past the water line. A cloud of gnats ascended to assail them that had disturbed the deep, and with the gnats came a stench of swollen meat and festered gases like the reek of Hell itself. In the shadow of the grass the dog whined. They paid neither the gnats nor the stench nor the dog any heed, bent already to the second body and hauling it up by the shoulders. The girl held the man steady while the old woman shifted the legs until the knees caught and held the rim. Together they lifted his back and pitched him headlong into the well. They did the same for the last body, and the cloud of gnats followed in a descending vortex like a school of fish chasing a proffered meal. The dog whined.

The women returned to the trampled and bloodstained clearing to collect their piles. They stuffed what they could into the haversack then slung the straps of the sack over two of the rifles like poles for a spit. The old woman hung the third rifle crossways over her shoulder, the strap bisecting her pendulous breasts, then both women bent and rested the rifle-ends on their shoulders to raise the heavy haversack slung between them. The girl in the lead and carrying the musket and cane pike while the old woman steadied their load. Neither had said one word the entire time, all their deeds by habit unspoken.

They jogged like this through the marsh, the sack swinging between them, their bodies slick with sweat and their thin stained shifts clinging to their thighs, until they reached a low-roofed hut thatched and camouflaged in the marsh reeds, the door barely tall enough to crouch through. Inside they tossed their collection onto a small but similar pile near the door, which the girl arranged hastily while the old woman stepped out the back and dipped a tin cup into a barrel of water and drank deeply, the water running in streaks down her dusty neck. The girl joined her and did the same, then they each drank again. The old woman left a splash in the bottom of her cup and tipped her head to pour the last down the back of her neck, while the girl returned indoors and braced the hut's small door ajar then lifted a hatch in the roof with a pole and propped it open. They both collapsed panting onto a rickety pallet bed with a thin lumpy mattress stuffed with grasses, the pillows toward the rear and their feet aimed at the door, the open hatch directly overhead for the meager breeze it offered. They left the mosquito net open. It was only late afternoon when they began to doze, but the heat and the murder had taken them and they slept side by side the night through.

Once, the older woman rose and staggered out the low door and squatted in the weeds to piss, and she thought she heard a rumble of cannon and cocked her head like an owl's to better discern the direction of the sound, but when she did so she caught the faint flicker of lightning out in the distant clouds, knew it for nature from the pale blue hue, so distinct from the devilish yellow of firelight or the orange flash of gunpowder. She held a hand into the air to test it but the wind was wrong. There might be rain but none to come their direction. She swiped at herself with the hem of her shift and waddled back inside to sleep again til dawn.

II

When day rose in a fog over the marsh they were awake already, resetting their crawfish traps and bringing in the wash they'd abandoned the day before. The air had stilled in the night and they could hear a few quiet birds uncertain in their songs. A handful of California gulls drifted inland from the beaches south. Once, the warble of a masked booby. Little else. The women sat just outside their doorway and nibbled on dry biscuits, sometimes picking out the mealworms. When they'd eaten, they pulled out their goods and arranged them in the patch of earth before the hut, sorted and packed them carefully into the haversack and an old rucksack. They kept nothing for themselves, the soldiers' own supply lines long bereft of anything the women didn't already have. In the load they now prepared they had three rifles, one a repeater though broken in some way they couldn't decipher, as well as a spare smoothbore musket, and each woman strapped on the shoulderarms to make a wide X across her bosom, then each hefted a pack onto her back. They took up their own arms, now cleaned save the stain of blood that would never leave the sharpened pole, and they hiked slowly into the marsh, feeling their path on instinct through the marsh toward the deeper bayou beyond.

The bayou was rimmed in occasional cypress hung heavy with a curtain of moss. The sun filtered through ocher and dark green, and the muddy shallows trapped among the roots wavered sickly in the light. All manner of putrid life slewed unseen in the muck. The women skirted the rim and walked along the spotty treeline until they came to a slender bar of moss-carpeted clay humped out of the bayou and tapering into the brackish interior. They held their weapons perpendicular like circus artists on a tightrope and walked swiftly along the narrow ridge of earth until they came to a shallow lake, a lonesome cypress rising from water at the edge, a tribe of woody knees surrounding the trunk like a congregation. These they navigated into the lake to a tiny island knotted with the roots of an oak tree. And so they progressed across the shallow lake. The air was damp and heavy, and their hair hung flat in their eyes but they did not need to see, so often had they come this way in the last three years. They took their time and trusted their feet, and at length they found a rotting wooden plank that led from a knee of root to a shabby boardwalk. They alit on the walk and followed its zigzagging path to the shack they sought.

They rested against the shambles of the dark wood shack and the old woman beat at the door with the side of her fist. Clovis, you in there? She pounded again. Come on, where you at? They heard a groan from the shack that could have been a man but might as easily have been the shack itself, but the groan was succeeded by a rolling belch, and the old woman shook her head and pushed on through the door.

Clovis sat in a cane chair leaned against the side wall. His shirt was loose and open over his hollow chest and he'd cut the legs of his underwear at the knees to let his skinny calves breathe. He was picking his teeth with a slender dagger as they entered, but when the thin light fell in a loose rectangle over him he looked up and smiled, raised the small bowl from which he drank his whiskey. Behind him, arrayed in what to him must have made sense, stood counters and shelves stacked with various accoutrements. A rack of firearms on the back wall and beside them a lumped pile of feed bags and flour sacks from which flour sifted through holes in the seams to form tiny white cones on the damp wood floor. A shelf with twice-read newspapers reshuffled and folded new. Beside them mildewed books, a small case of straight razors and on a counter near the shelf a motley display of tin cups, hammered tin plates and oxidizing cutlery. A cluster of barrels in the corner draped in a wide canvas cloth but reeking of home-distilled whiskey. A decrepit black gimp slouched against the barrels with his eyes rolling aimlessly in his skull, his huge head wallowing against the canvas and his mouth open for no apparent reason.

Clovis eyed the women and took a long sloppy drink from his bowl, then set it aside and leered at them. Got me something good? he said, and without further word the women set their loads on the floor and unstrapped the firearms and opened the packs. He gored muck from under his fingernails with the tip of the dagger as he watched them. When they'd finished they stepped away and waited. He tipped forward his chair and hauled the bags closer. He hefted one of the rifles and cocked it then let down the hammer and nodded, but when he picked up the smoothbore he grunted and tossed both shoulderarms into the corner. He bent to root through the packs but only tilted a few items to peer beneath them. He flipped shut the flap on the rucksack and kicked the haversack with his bare toes. This is shit, he said. This the best you can get for old Clovis?

This is all they is and you know it, the old woman said.

It's as good as we ever got, the girl said, but the old woman put a hand on her arm.

All you ever got was shit. Hell, petites, I can't use none of this. It'd be a hassle just to keep it in my store.

People's gonna need this stuff, the woman said.

Clovis stood up, tottering over them, then he stretched his arms akimbo with his fists on his bony hips as though to steady himself on himself. He eyed them both then shook his head.

New Orleans was taken two years ago, some say General Lovell done run off crying. Them Yankees took Fort DeRussey too. They running now, I hear, had us a good win up in Mansfield, but the Yankees turned it right around in Natchitoches and they's beating us still even while retreating. It don't make no difference either way anymore. They pulled Grant out these parts and sent him to Virginia. War's in the east. We done down in these parts, far as I's concerned. Won't be but just skirmishes now. He spat into the corner and bent to collect his bowl. I got no more customers to sell this shit to. He tipped his bowl and drank.

This shit you call it come to you all but free anyway, Clovis. You'll turn a dollar on it somehow no matter where the war's at. Come on, vieux, just make a bill.

Clovis scratched his chin then drained his bowl and slung

it into the back of the shop. He kicked at the gimp by the barrels. Hey boy, get your nigger ass up and clear this junk. The gimp rolled his eyes over the two packs then tottered toward them and dragged them by their straps around a counter. Clovis sauntered toward the shelf near his chair and pulled up a floorboard and withdrew a plain box. He lifted the lid and started riffling through crumpled bills.

My eye! the woman said. You ain't handing us no money and you know it. We want food, you old bastard.

He chuckled and tossed the box onto the chair, a few bills of paper fluttering forgotten to the floor. Ok, ok, he said. He went to the back by the stacks of rifles and rummaged in the pile of feed sacks. He brought a heavy bag of rice and a sack of flour, and he chucked the food at their feet. Each a one, he said. This here's good stuff. Get you a roux going and you be set for anything.

You got any coffee? the girl said.

Clovis laughed loud to shake the roofbeams and clapped his chest. Shit, child, when you see coffee last? Go talk to the Yankees. I got me some yaupon leaves you're welcome to, if you wanted to brew you some tea.

Shit, the woman said. Keep it. We'll just keep on brewing acorns.

The two women hefted their sacks and turned to shuffle out into the bayou. Clovis sat in his chair and leaned it against the wall again, but he called out to them as they crossed his threshold.

Now stay youself there, boo. You want you a little more? Maybe some of this old bust head? He hefted a jug and decanted into his bowl, then held it out on offer. Come on in here the both of you and stay a while. Stay the night, maybe. He winked at them and licked his lips.

The hell you say, the old woman said. I'd never with a old drunken bastard the likes of you.

He laughed and leaned back on the wall and slurped from his bowl as they turned again to the bayou.

III

Dusk shadowed the reed bed and the sky gloomed red like fired iron, and while the cicadas set in and far off the frogs began a song, a spectral figure emerged hat and shoulders from the rippled surface of the backwaters. He carried a long walking stick with which he plumbed the path before him, and tied to the top of the stick hung a heavy black sack. He pushed his way through the weedy murk and emerged onto the damp ground of the reed beds dripping and naked save the wide black hat on his head. He leaned against the stick and felt his flesh in the last red light, picked a few dangling leeches like mutant teats from his wiry thighs and knotted buttocks. Then he untied the sack, which revealed itself as a preacher's cassock, and unrolled from within it a heavy Bowie knife, a small tin match safe, a leather pouch and a string of beads. He removed the hat and hung it atop a stand of reeds, then he draped himself in the cassock, tied his waist and hung the beads from the front of the rope belt. He tucked the match safe and the pouch in his pocket and he slipped the knife into the rope at his back. He donned the hat and inspected the sky and the dark ground before him, then he struck out through unseen trails in the reeds. He meandered for some time, the night falling heavy around him til he could no longer distinguish the hem of his cassock from the black ground below it. His own hands seemed to float in space like incorporeal spirits guiding him through the marsh. At last he pushed aside the reeds like curtains and stepped into a small clearing, in the back of which nestled a hut. A drift of smoke rose from a lifted hatch, the smoke less dark than the darkness around it. He looked around the clearing but saw no other markers, and he checked the sky for his bearings but could make out no stars for guidance. He bent low to the ground and laid his stick gently there, then slipped the knife from the rope and crept up on the hut.

He pushed in without knocking to interrupt the women at their meal. They looked up at him, one with her mouth full and the other just taking a bite. The girl fell sideways across the floor and grabbed for a bayonet, but the woman exclaimed to stop her: Buford! What the hell you doing here? And dressed like that!

He crouched under the shallow ceiling with the knife still tight in his fist, but on hearing the old woman, he set to laughing, a demented cackle of disbelief, and he staggered further into the hut. Heaven or Hell, I must be dead. He shook his head and laughed some more. I's hungry. Gimme some that food and I'll tell you all about it.

The woman gestured at the girl. Go on, get him a plate. Buford reeled again and dragged over an upturned bucket and sat down. He kept at the laugh gone weary.

I can't believe you made it back, the old woman said. The

war over?

The girl brought him a large earthenware mug filled with watery unseasoned rice sprinkled with tiny shrimps no bigger than a thumbnail. Where's Remy, Buford? Where's my husband?

Buford had his lips over the rim and was shoveling the food from the cup with his fingers, tilting back as he ate. When he spoke, he spoke around the food. Hold on I'll get to it.

Come on, answer the girl. Where ma fils? The woman wagged a finger at him. I don't like you coming back without him.

I ain't come back, I done absquatulated.

You deserted? Left my boy, my only son, out they in that war?

The woman snatched the cup from him but he reached and grabbed it back, upended it and tapped out the last of the food, then handed it to the girl.

Gimme some water.

The girl moved but the old woman stopped her with a hand on her arm. Buford eyed them both.

I ain't left him, Buford said. But he ain't coming.

Start at the start, the woman said.

We was with that outfit come through and rounded us up, but whatever fool was running it got us all but wiped out, so we got pulled into the Third Arkansas. We shuffled around a bit and after we lost New Orleans, Remy and me got split up but found each other again at Port Hudson, and we stuck together after. We was a few days north up at Mansfield and licking Grant good when they turned on us, whooping us on the run, and then just three days back your Remy got kilt. Head shot clean through—

He stopped and shook his head. The girl dipped him some

water in the same cup as his supper; he downed it in a toss and handed it back. She got him another, and he took it and held it. You got any whiskey?

My son is dead?

Yes'm, he mustered out. And that was it for me. I lit out of they in a hurry, slipped down into the trees and made south. Ain't no sense in none of this no more. Hell, I don't even remember why we fighting. Not like this war would of ever done folks like us any good anyhows. All we ever did was kill some Yanks and march around and kill some more Yanks then get kilt ourselves.

How'd Remy come to get shot? the girl said, but Buford took a long time answering.

Ain't no kind of war out they I ever heard about. They's one time I was out on patrol of a evening and I come upon a couple of Yankees shitting in the bushes, and I just slipped up on them and slit they throats right they in the bushes. They pants was still around they ankles. The second one tried to get out his pistol but I just slit his throat too, cool as you please, and they both fell over and died in they own shit.

Buford shook his head, downed the cup of water.

I ain't even think nothing of it til I got back to camp, never reported it or nothing, and then all that night I had the shakes like you wouldn't believe. Never slept a wink. Hell, I reckon I might not of slept these last two years but when I was drunk, and that was sure not ever often enough. You sure you ain't got no whiskey?

But what about my son?

I told you. Shot through the head up near Mansfield. I don't even know who by. Can't tell one side from the other anymore. We wasn't even fighting. Remy and me hung back from the battle and tried to keep out of it but this damned lieutenant found us and rode up on us, chased us all over that battlefield, our own officer, til finally we had to dive us into the river and swim for it. That lieutenant was crazier'n shit, went to snarling and barking after us, came down that damn riverbank on all fours I swear to the Lord. Took some shots at us but all he hit was water. All down the river we could hear him screaming, howling like a rabid dog. We all got a little wild out they, but this'n? Shoot. We ain't never eat nothing but tack, never had no proper meal what I ever saw, but this lieutenant, he had hisself some meat or other and fairly regular, though none ever dared ask where he got it cause often as not he'd eat his meat raw, and it never was a pleasant sight. He what we was running from as much as the war itself. He was that war, the whole nonsensical mess of it all balled up in that—

My Remy, the old woman said.

Buford looked at her, wiped his heavy lower lip and smelled the back of his hand. Anyways, he said, we got downstream a piece and waded out the rest of the way. We hid out in some thicket that night and then hiked off in the morning. We come to a old gatehouse on some plantation or other and we was hungry so we slipped in to find us some food, but it was all gone. They ain't no food nowheres anymore. Remy, he got mad and kicked up a table and that's when somebody popped up from a hole in the floor and started shooting. For all I know it was another soldier, ours or theirs, had hisself the same idea we did and just beat us to it. Got Remy in the back of the head and his face just billowed out like—

Buford looked from one woman to the other and closed his eyes, shook his head.

I dove through the window. I's lucky to get out of they alive, shots all through the trees while I ran.

For a long while it was quiet in the hut. The woman's face went wet with tears but she said nothing. The girl stared at the earthen floor and pulled her arms around herself. To no one in particular she whispered, My husband is dead. Then she looked at her mother-in-law. My husband is dead.

Buford withdrew the pouch from his cassock, unrolled it and dug inside to produce a small clay pipe full of dry tobacco. He tucked away the pouch and leaned to pull a stick from the small fire, lit the pipe and sat smoking. The woman wiped her cheek and looked hard at Buford. What happened to that man come and conscripted you two? That Georgia bastard?

He got kilt almost soon as we left the bayou. Wasn't even the war that got him, it was a whore. He tried to get out of paying on account of he was a officer in the great Confederacy and she decided not to abide it, so she shot him in the belly as he left. He took forever to die, too, come crawling back into camp holding some of his own guts in his fist like it was boudin. Crying and carrying on. Surgeon tried to stitch him up but he done bled too much as it was. Bout glowed in the dark when he came on us, he was so pale. He died that same night but he was miserable doing it.

Good, the girl said. The son of a bitch. They both looked at her. Well he was. He deserved to die like that, carrying off my husband.

The old woman looked at Buford.

They come and took you boys off so fast we was left wondering what to do. Weren't hardly no food to start with, with the chickens not laying no more and the one cow drying up, bad almost then as now. I was so awaiting the day he'd come home to us.

She looked at Buford's bare feet. Now it just you.

Buford surveyed the dim hut, the shallow iron pan of steaming rice and shrimp. Shoot, you don't mind my saying, but I thought you'd of rebuilt by now. How long ago was them storms what knocked over your house?

Ages, the woman said. They was hail last summer. You believe that? Hail in the damn summer all the way down here. Like God's own joke. The world turned inside out so's Hell we live in now and Heaven done buried below us.

Ain't no one left to help us, the girl said. You know all mine are gone or still in the Carolinas, and Mother's kin back in the delta, well.

We could do the work, the woman added, but this here's the only house I know to build, and that just from stories my grandmere used to tell.

I know how hard it must of been out here and it's just a damned miracle you two is even alive, Buford said. He gestured at the pot of rice. Them little shrimps is easy enough to come by if you walk far enough to the shore, but you ain't growing no rice out here nor raising no other crops. What y'all doing for food?

We done turned beggar, the girl said. Ain't nothing else for it.

He eyed them both. Who you begging from? Ain't no one left in this here marsh, all the men gone off to fight and most everyone else absconded for safer parts. Even if they was anyone here, ain't no one got no food anyways. I know, I must of broke into ever place in the whole of Vermillion Parish.

You learn to eat what you might not want to. We've ate rats, snakes, even some stewed cicadas when times was real hard.

Yeah, but that they rice don't grow itself and ain't no fields near here. You can't live as hard as y'all's telling and have rice to put your shrimps in. His eyes lingered over the half-covered musket and the bayonet blade that lay nearby where the girl had dropped it. Y'all been stealing too?

You shut your mouth, the girl said.

Buford raised both hands in apology. I ain't making no judgment, I's just wondering in case they's anything good left for me.

You look like you already found youself a charity, the old woman said. Them's priests clothes you wearing, I know it.

They is and it weighs on me hard. I ain't kilt him, though. Found him bathing in a creek, these draped in a bush, and needs must when the Devil drives. I couldn't go walking around in my uniform for fear of getting pulled back in, and people trust a preacher no matter they faith. I could walk right up to a officer of either army and shake his hand and no one would try and reenlist me or shoot me or nothing. Made getting back here a sure sight easier, I tell you.

Now you're back, what'll you do? the girl said.

I ain't reckoned. My place still standing?

I don't know, the woman said. I ain't been out they since you left. We had us a hell of a storm last fall, might of been a hurricane, even. Could be the roof's gone or it flooded, I don't know.

Well, shoot, then, I suppose I ought to go have a looksee. I'll be back over, though, get y'all settled before I start in on my own.

We put this here together without no help and it works just fine, the woman said. Rebuilds easier than any house, too. Ain't no need for you to come round here for that.

Well, I do thank you both for the meal and I's sorry I had to bring you the news I did.

That's the last we can spare, Buford, the woman said. I's sorry, too, but we can't feed you again.

Shoot, y'all ain't much for neighborliness no more, is you.

These last years they weren't no neighbors, and now they ain't the means for sharing. We can't look out for others if we ain't here to do the looking.

I understand. He looked from woman to girl, rubbed the nape of his neck. And like I said I appreciate it.

He stood from the bucket and cracked his head against the center pole of the roof, then he stumbled again toward the door and out into the night.

The women sat still on their stools and watched the door and listened to the cicadas singing. After a while the woman looked to her widowed daughter-in-law and said, What's the matter with you?

I don't know, she said.

You's awful quiet.

I know it. I guess I'm just sad is all.

You and me alike, but sad don't get the dishes done.

IV

Buford's shack had fallen off its thick cypress blocks and listed rhomboid in the reeds, one wall sagging into the water. In the night it looked like some hulking fabrication of the marsh slinking back into the muck whence it had come. He approached the good side with his knife in his fist, crouching below the window then craning his neck to peer over the sill. He held his breath. He half-expected to find the crazed lieutenant hunkered inside, panting like a dog, Buford a bone he longed to dig up. Or worse. There were stories he never believed but would consider now: The blazing eyes of a rougarou leering yellow through the paneless frame. The werewolf of the bayou, the hot breath through its dripping teeth the breath of the swamp itself.

He saw nothing inside but smelled it nonetheless, a rot of flesh and fur though it was the stench of ordinary decay, nothing supernatural about it. He slid down an embankment into water up his ankles and wrenched askew the broken door. He crouched and waited. He heard a scuttle and whine then felt the matted fur of a small dog scuff past his foot, but he kept immobile. When nothing else moved, he reached the match safe from his pocket and popped aflame a match on the doorframe. The interior of the shack wavered in the yellow light like it was underwater. A wreck of moldering reeds in one corner, the scent of scat by the wall that cantered into the marsh. His lantern bent and glassless still hung on a nail by the door, but it was drained and wickless. Some shards of crockery. Nothing else remained. His few utensils, his table and two chairs and his bedframe, his old cookstove, everything pillaged. The match expired on his thumbtip and he hissed. He shuffled into the corner where he'd seen the pile of reeds, kicked at it and heard the scuttle of insects. When his eyes had readjusted to the dark, he stirred the nest with his walking stick til he was satisfied whatever had called it home had now absconded, then he kicked the reeds together again and fell atop the loose mat to sleep. But no sleep arrived, and he lay instead for some hours just staring upward into nothing.

Sometime near midnight he woke screaming to flashes in the dark and covered his head and scurried into a corner, but when the concussion came it was only the rumble of thunder. He rolled upright and leaned against the wall, hugging himself with his knees against his chest. When the lightning flashed it showed like teeth through the gaps in the roof planks, and he flinched each time the thunder followed, but after several minutes he caught his breath and stilled. A hollow pat tapped an uneven rhythm on the slanted rooftop, and soon the rain was drumming away. He began to cry quietly. The floor went damp in strips.

The rain went on for two days straight. Each house—Buford's shack and the low marsh hut where the women lived—lay quiet in the rain, where their inhabitants attended to what chores they could. Buford spread his cassock on the roof and covered it in reeds to slow the seepage indoors, and naked he worked on the house, prying loose the tilted side in the water one board at a time, hauling out barehanded what nails he could. He tore down the whole side, left just the one central stud to hold up the roof while he worked, then with the base of the decrepit lantern for a mallet he hammered up a makeshift wall. Hoped it would hold through the weather until he could dismantle the whole mess and start clean on higher ground.

At their hut the women went out each wet morning and each steamy evening to muck the marsh for risen crawfish and anything else that might escape in the fallacious safety of the storm. Each wondered if the other was crying but it was hard to tell in the rain and neither spoke of the deceased Remy, or indeed of much else. Indoors they boiled roots and crawfish and waterbugs and sipped the hot stew, dared not open their sacks of grain as the water dripped through gaps in the reed roof, and they tried not to look at each other, each lost in her thoughts. On the second afternoon the old woman stepped out back to the rain barrel and shut the door and stayed there a long time. When she came in the girl noticed dirt under the woman's ragged nails but she said nothing of it, and soon the old woman had sprawled like a dead crab on the mattress and was breathing in an abnormal rhythm though she did not sleep. Neither slept much, and always they listened for drifters or nearby skirmishes, but none arrived.

The morning hot already in the early summer, the girl sat out on a shallow plank by the water, scrubbing laundry in a bucket.

The wind had left with the storm and the air hung heavy as her hair, limp in her eyes, and she kept sweeping it back to see. After one such swipe she spied Buford, shirtless, wading up through the shallows, his shadow stretched long before him. He carried a cane pole and a string of two small fish. When he reached her he slung the pole over his shoulder and draped the fish on it as he cocked a foot up onto the plank. He'd tied the cassock into pantaloons around his legs, and they draped heavy from his bare knees, dripping on the plank. His shadow covered her and slipped out into the water. He said nothing, just watched her rub and wring her laundry, but she paid him no attention. Finally, he spat into the marsh and stood tall again.

Fine summer day out in the bayou. Even the skeeters is resting. He gazed at her openly as she rocked to and fro with the wash. A body could near forget they's a war on.

The girl didn't look at him but she spoke. Them's some nice little fish you got there. They good for eating?

They just a couple bullhead, good enough for one as ain't got none. What about y'all? What's y'all doing for food these days? He looked around him as though to find some hidden store in the reeds. You ain't farming. I been all around these parts the last few days and ain't seen no plots.

Nothin'll grow out here and you know it.

Buford nodded and licked his thick lips. Uh huh, uh huh. You know, when I was in camp, they was this sutler, this fella sold all sorts of things, stuff you wasn't supposed to be able to get no more, least not in camp. He brought in coffee, by God, coffee and some old popskull and one time he had this picture of a naked lady, not some drawing but one of them photographs, her all splayed on a bed undressed and her legs spread. I don't mean to offend, but that's the world we's in now. That old boy got hisself rich, I'm telling you.

He leaned against the plank again, one foot up and his free arm on his knee.

You know how he done it? He was stealing. Everbody out they is stealing. That the only way to survive anymore, even in the army. I stole from that sutler what he done stole to sell us, and sometimes others'd steal it off me. Ain't no shame in wartime.

He dipped his head to catch her eye. She glanced at him but kept on at the washing.

That's what y'all been up to, ain't it? Stealing some? She ignored him. Come on now, tell me where y'all is getting it and maybe I can help some.

Like you helped my husband? The girl dropped her rags and looked at him directly. Buford stood back and scratched his head. Why'd you leave Remy there in that house to die?

I didn't leave him to die, he was already dead. I just left him, same as you would've.

She resumed her wash with greater fervor, wrestling the cloth more than cleaning it.

You pining for him? That it?

You shut up about him.

You must of been thinking about it lately. Since I come back. What you gonna do now he's dead? You can't stay here with that old woman. You young and healthy and have your own self to think about. Your own needs.

You mind your mouth, you hear?

He ran his tongue over his heavy lower lip and smiled at her.

You could mind it for me. How's about you come on over to my place? I got room for you.

They heard a rustle in the reeds and he looked up as the girl resumed her wash. The old woman approached with a fresh basket, and he watched her come. The early morning light through the heads of the reeds cut ocher stripes across her face so it flickered as she walked. He waved at her when she was near.

Say, I was just telling how it's a fine day out. Not too hot yet.

Buford, what the hell you doing over here and down in the water? You want a visit you come on up to the house like normal folk.

He hefted the rod at her, the catfish dangling loose on either side of the pole. Why, I was catching some fish. Man's gotta eat, you know. He smiled at her and gestured with the pole. I suppose woman's gotta eat, too.

She sneered at him, but he laughed and flicked the pole so the fish tumbled onto the plank.

Y'all take these. Repay you for your kindness the other night.

What about you? the girl said.

I'll go catch me some more. He turned and waded back up the water, his knees coming up high to clear the weeds and muck below. The girl looked from the fish back at the woman.

Go on take it, the woman said. Ain't polite nor smart to turn down good food when it's offered. Then she herself grabbed up the fish. These look all right. Bit small but good enough for us. She turned them glistening in the heavy light, and then looked down at the girl. What was y'all talking about?

Nothing. Just the weather like he said. How hot it's going to get later.

You stay clear that son of a bitch. He ain't even sorry he come back alone. For all we know he kilt our Remy hisself, if Remy even dead. Ain't no better than a Yankee. She spat in near the same spot as Buford had and watched him waddle heron-legged away. Then she saw him whip his head to look across the water at the same time she herself heard the sound. The gallop of horse hooves as two cavalry riders rode into the marsh, one in blue and the other gray, though between sweat and dust you could hardly tell them apart. One had his saber out and whipped his horse with it, fleeing the other who aimed a long-barreled pistol and fired but missed.

Buford and the women watched the contest unfold, their various errands arrested. As the riders neared the water, the pursuer fired again and the swordsman fell from his horse without a sound. He scrambled up to run hands and knees like an ape as the pistoleer fired again, but nothing happened. Even at that distance they could see him check his weapon but it was empty. He threw it at the scrambling man, then he drew his own saber and jumped from his horse. The wounded man scuttled to his feet and they met standing, their swords flashing in the sunlight. Over the water the thrusts were silent but the parries sounded almost like whipcracks. One nearly slashed the other but lost his balance, then they both rushed in close and grappled with their spare hands on each other's hilts until they fell sidelong into the water. They came up waist deep and sputtering but slashed at the water as they wiped their faces and they continued their duel. Buford was wading sideways back toward the women, his eyes keen on the fight. They glanced at him but kept their focus on the cavalrymen.

The swordfight drifted closer as one tried again to flee the other, and by the time they'd reached the middle of the pond, they had to raise their arms almost over their heads just to strike. Buford had reached the women and was standing beside them at the plank. The soldiers were sputtering and half-choking in the marsh now, and both had seen the spectators on the shore and both began to call for help. They swung again, each flailing and splashing until, with a blind wild swipe, one gashed the other across the face. Even from the shore and amid the thrashing in the water, the spectators heard the crack of his cheekbone, and a spray of blood arced out from his severed nose. He collapsed on his back to float away in the marsh. The victor panting and spitting out water dog-paddled to the bank, crying for help as he, too, was wounded, was in fact the man who'd been shot. As he approached, Buford held out his hand and the cavalryman grabbed it, but Buford holding tight to the man's free arm jabbed a sharp punch and broke his nose, then he gripped the officer's collar and forced him underwater. The shallow water roiled with their struggle as Buford plunged him like laundry and sometimes loosed his grip on the collar to punch the man in the face, cursing and spitting the while, his teeth showing to the gums. The girl said, God Amighty, loud enough for Buford to hear, and when he looked their direction he shouted for the women to go after the man floating away. They dropped their wash and the string of fish and jumped feet first into the water as though they'd been awaiting permission.

When they reached the other man and took hold of him, he writhed and spat blood in the air like a surfaced dolphin, and they exclaimed together, Hell he's still alive! They both dunked him under, a shoulder apiece, and drowned him as well. When he'd gone limp in the water they hauled the corpse to the shore, where Buford already was stripping his dead solider and tossing the clothes to the bank. He was hissing in the form of words, Goddamn sonofabitch, over and over with each exhaled breath. When the women reached him he pointed across the water to the horses and their saddlebags.

To hell with them fish, we'll all eat good now. Look at all that gear on them horses and hell, the horses themselves.

The girl nodded and said, not with joy but as if to inventory what they'd yet to see, I bet there's mess kits and blankets and ammunition and who knows what else in them saddlebags.

The horses stood calm by the water, one with his head dipped to drink.

The old woman made no comment, bent as she was to her work. Buford seethed still and had torn two buttons from the trousers. The girl touched his arm and he looked at her hand there. He refused to look at her, but he moved with greater deliberation and the trousers came loose from the dead man's hips.

They worked side by side and finished the bodies and piled the clothes then kicked the men back into the water to float away.

V

Buford sat on a stool in the bayou store, the cassock open over his naked chest, sorting through the saddlebags and hauling out various items: a bullseye canteen, two wooden canteens, two watches, a photograph of a young woman, a stack of assorted mess dishes and cookpots, some firestarters and flints, two blankets, a crumpled gray kepi and a dark blue slouch hat, a stropping belt and two knives. There had been five, but he'd kept one for himself and the women took the two folding knives. Against the wall beside him leaned two carbines, a Spencer and a Maynard, and the pair of cavalry sabers in their steel scabbards. On the small table beside him lay three singleshot smoothbore pistols and two Colt revolvers, one an 1851 and the other a fine blued 1860. Opposite him sat Clovis leaning on his knee, his face down as he eyed the goods and grunted, unhappy with having to deal with a man, much less with having to admit the supply was worth good money. Buford finished his own inventory and stuffed a few things back into the pack then sat back and smiled. In the back, the gimp lolled and hummed some tune to himself, and tucked into a corner lazed a drunken, naked whore with her back to them, the twin moons of her great ass pink in the stovelight. Clovis shook his head and retreated into the dark rear of the store. Buford rubbed his chin and traced one finger over his bottom lip as he looked at the ass of the whore. Clovis returned and set down a sack of rice and one of flour, then he shuffled away and came back with two more sacks, these of beans and okra, as well as two small sacks of salt and sugar. Buford eyed them without moving.

This all they is?

All the farms is run dry and the supply trains don't get out this way at all. I's lucky to of come upon even this much.

Shit, I ain't choosey. You can bring me some whiskey to make up the difference.

Whiskey's worth more'n this food I already give you.

The hell it is, I know you just brew this stuff out back yourself. And you forgetting about them horses I said I'd bring you.

How's I supposed to get horses out the bayou to sell?

I reckon the same way them horses got in the bayou. Can't be at all hard for a man of your means and cunning.

They eyed each other. Finally Buford grunted and handed back the sack of sugar.

Alright, fine, I don't need no sugar anyhow. Now bring me a jug, and don't water it none.

Clovis returned with a heavy jug and two tin cups. He poured a measure of whiskey into each and they sat together and drank. Buford held up the small photograph to the lantern light and handed it to Clovis.

That's a fine carte de visite, Clovis said. Who you reckon she is?

I don't know, but she's one of our fine ladies. I pulled her out of the beehive our boy was carrying.

Clovis traced his finger over the picture's face.

She a beauty. He aimed his thumb at the naked woman behind them. That whore Marceline, she good to look at but she meaner'n a kicked dog. I keep her drunk most of the time just to keep her quiet. They drank apiece, Buford staring at the whore Marceline's ass. Then Clovis smiled: How about them two out they in the marsh with you? You managed anything that direction?

It's early days. I just come back.

Clovis nodded, washed back his drink, poured another and topped up Buford's cup as well.

What battles you seen before you come back to us?

I seen as few as I could but more than I cared to. It's been a hell of a year.

It weren't always so.

No sir, year before was a fine year. I was with the Western Louisiana under General Taylor, we licked them Yankees up and down the bayou like you wouldn't believe. They couldn't fart but we was on them in a hellstorm of bullets. They was this one company, I didn't know them but I fought with them from time to time, they took to killing the Yankee's dogs when we run through a camp. These boys was crazy, crazier still before old Taylor showed up, they'd cut the faces off them dogs. I mean skin them clean, fur and all, and they'd dry them into masks. They'd tie those old dog faces over they heads and charge howling into battle. I ain't talking like that old rebel yell the way them yellowhammers do it over in Alabama, I mean a goddamn howl. They called themselves the Rougarou Corps, like to scared the hell out all of us, not just the Yankees. But Taylor didn't take kindly to them, and after Port Hudson fell and we all marched back up Bayou Teche, he was in a sore mood and he disbanded the whole company, sent them scattered through the other troops and told them to burn they masks. One of them boys took command of my own company and he was a son of a bitch, I can tell you.

What he do?

Shit, that lieutenant? Name of Whelan, he weren't in this war for any reason I'd of recognized. He just liked to kill. They was this one time, we'd licked the Yankees so good half of them ain't even had time to run off, and we wound up with some two dozen prisoners, even some of them nigger troops they trussed up.

God Amighty.

Afterward, the general set up some hospital tents and put them Yankees in to rest up for a march, cause they was all wounded some way or other, and we encamped for the night. But they was these screams all in the night, not nothing we ain't heard before but they was so much of it that some of us went to have a looksee. And they was Whelan and a couple of boys from his old unit, them rougarous, they playing some foot ball out in the moonlight, and when we come up on them we seen they was kicking around a head. I mean one them Yankee's heads, cut clean off and rolling out they in the grass.

Go to bed.

I tell it true, and it was just one among many—them boys gone into the tents that night and cut the heads off ever one of them Yankees, stacked over on a side like artillery balls. Next morning the general found them all and like to tore our whole camp upside down looking for who done it, but ain't none of us was gonna tell it. Not with Whelan standing they watching us. He'd of kilt us all if he thought it would serve him. Like to kill me when I run off.

Clovis looked at him. Buford looked at the whore Marceline's ass in the back of the store.

They counted them heads before burying them, and they weren't all accounted for. Far's I know they's still some missing.

Clovis poured himself a third drink but Buford held his hand over his own cup, and when Clovis set down the jug, Buford bent to move it behind his stool. Clovis eyed it, then shrugged and drank.

You lucky you made it back at all, crazy wolf-soldiers or otherwise. Come a time you and me might be the only men left in these parts.

Buford nodded, looked around and sipped the last splash of whiskey in his cup.

This here's a nice shop you keep. Little run down but I bet you do all right.

Clovis laughed. I do fine long as the war lasts. I hope them Yankees never give up after us. He raised his cup but it was empty, and he leaned forward looking into it as though to divine something in the oily sheen at the bottom. Won't be long yet, though, I reckon. Too many dead, ain't enough really to carry on this war.

Oh they's years left in this war. You watch. Yanks won't quit fighting til they win, and we won't quit til ever one of us is dead. No, they'll keep at it til they can't go no more. It's a kind of business with them, at this point. War's all either country knows, and everthing seems to depend on it now.

Indeed, Clovis said. He sniffed his cup and shook a last drop into his tilted mouth. Buford clapped his knees and rose and collected his sacks. He spied a brace of ducks hanging from the wall as he stood, and he lifted them down.

Clovis frowned then rubbed the back of his head. I'll account them ducks on credit, for the horses, but you be sure and bring in some good stuff next time you come.

As Buford stepped out along the wooden walk into the bayou, he came upon two sad figures, a half-crippled old woman muddy with filth and her young granddaughter, not nine years old, all but naked and hung with rags like moss on a tree. The grandmother was bent double under a bundle of goods with a mud-stained pistol like a relic from the Revolution and a ruined sword hilt sticking out of the bundle. They froze when they saw him, and when he stopped as well they scurried back from him, wary. He nodded and edged around them and walked on, turning back once to see them scuttle down the boards and duck into Clovis's shop.

That evening they sat together in the women's hut where they shared a meal of watery duck gumbo. The old woman had baked a flat, dry bread, and they tore hunks of it loose to soak up the broth and chewed with the juices falling over their chins. Buford was drinking his whiskey from a cup and kept passing the jug to the old woman, but she waved him off. Toward the end, they tipped their bowls and slurped at the last of the okra and nibblets of duck. When the broth was gone from his bowl, Buford abandoned the bread and held the bowl under his chin and shoveled in the remains with his fingers. The girl took a pair of iron tongs by the fire and fished a duck bone from the steaming pot and sat sucking on it. Buford was beginning to get drunk, and he watched the girl as she slurped the duckmeat from the bone. The old woman tore a fresh hunk of bread and took to wiping the walls of her bowl with it. When she'd finished she reached and took Buford's bowl and wiped it with the bread as well. Buford belched and sat back and poured another drink to sip.

Clovis has got hisself a good old business, ain't he?

The women ate without answering.

Army's running through rifles and sabers like crazy, but the real business? Shoot, the good money's in them clothes and boots, specially the boots. I remember I had to fight the same man twice just to keep the shoes I had and they wasn't even his size. I seen men get kilt just scouring the battlefield after, looking at Yankee feet and then getting shot by the damned chaplain reading they last rights. I seen men march into battle with two hats tied around they feet. I'd say the boots alone was worth half this here meal.

The women ate, ignoring him. He drank again and smiled.

Old Clovis, he says you two done him some good business. How many you kilt like the ones we kilt today?

The old woman barely paused between bites of bread to speak. That ain't none your business. You just mind your beeswax.

Shoot, you saw how good we was working together today. Why not let me join you? I seen battle, I can kill a man quick.

The girl chucked the stripped bone and pulled another from the pot. The old woman hammered her chest to belch, then looked at Buford.

You said youself old Clovis ain't complaining. We'll just stick to our own methods, and you can do as you please by your lonesome.

Buford leaned toward her, a splash of whiskey sluicing over the rim of the cup. I could be one of y'all, you know. He cocked his head toward the girl, spoke in a hoarse whisper. How's about you let me marry that one?

You're drunk, the girl said. You're talking balderdash. She stood up. We're pretty tuckered out, Buford, you go on home now. Back to your own place.

He laughed again but he hefted his jug on a finger and staggered out into the night muttering. Inside, the woman sat beside the girl.

That no-good son of a bitch. You watch out for that'n, girl. He after you. Eyes roaming places they've no business. Practically sniffing the air for you. You stay clear of him.

The girl glanced at her but said nothing nor ceased her eating.

Outside, Buford stumbled half-lost in the marsh, careening through the reed bed in a delirious jog. He came into a clearing that wasn't his own and he stood confused a moment before he recognized the abandoned lot by its well, an old joke among those who knew better. A sugarcaner from north of New Orleans had come into the bayou looking for new opportunity. He founded the mill where Remy and Buford once labored and built a sizeable home for his family, a wife and three daughters and yard of chickens and two cows and mongrel of a dog. But he was afraid of the bayou water and the detritus hidden under the skin of summer pollens, so he'd hired a team of men who laughed at him behind his back as they sank the useless well. The family lasted a year before the women left him and six months later he followed, leaving the big house barren with the doors open and the glass gone from the windows. Some of the siding on Buford's first home had come from the abandoned mansion, and Remy's father had pillaged the window frames for some purpose Buford never learned. Soon the only remnants were this denuded patch of earth and the hollow wall of the well.

Buford sauntered to the well and loomed over it, laughed and then shouted into its maw, but instead of an echo he was greeted by flies. He waved at them and lurched forward, then he caught the scent and almost fell in but managed to tilt himself sideways to vomit in the grass. He knelt there panting, looking at the well, for nearly half an hour, the shrouded moon sinking low on the distant prairie beyond the marsh. The starlight wan in the clouds. He pushed his fingers into the decrepit earth and finally crawled up and staggered home.

VI

Buford kicked loose his bed of old reeds and hefted aside the graying planks covering his former hearth. He ducked and reached up the plugged flue and yanked down a sack. He sorted the items within, select pieces he'd kept back from the two dead cavalrymen. He lifted the sack onto his shoulder and rounded the leaning remnants of his shack, behind which stood the restless horses. They shuffled in the dirt and when he reached for the reins of the nearest it whinnied and shied away from him, but he wooed it closer with his hand outheld, his fingers soft as his voice. He rubbed its muzzle and patted the neck of the other, then he flipped the sack onto one of the saddles and tied it to the horn and walked the horses away down the marsh toward the lake. They hesitated at the rim but he tugged them on in, slashing knee-deep through the waters and later their weight bowing the boardwalk that led to Clovis's store. He tied them to the post and left them blocking the only entrance in or out, and he bargained with Clovis for further goods: a smallish broadaxe and an adze, an auger, a black-headed claw hammer, a simple combination plane missing some of its blades, a rusting handsaw, an a-frame square, a sack of square nails and an assortment of mismatched hinges. A shovel, a bucket. Some cookpots and a few tin spoons, a castiron fireplace hook and matching tongs. Two suits of ill-fitting clothes and a needle and two spools of thread. A bolt of canvas mildewed at the edges. A fifty-foot coil of rope. A newish lantern and oil, a box of matches. Clovis offered to let him borrow a horse to haul his accessories home but he'd just have to bring the horse back, so Buford declined. He took back the sack now emptied and filled it, tied a fat knot in the mouth and rigged a sling from the rope, the loose ends looped over one arm, and lugged the sack onto his back and tightened the sling. He collected the ax and adze in one hand and the saw in the other and stooped out the door. He nearly fell into the rank water sidling past the horses, so little walk they left him, with their eyes wide and pleading, but they let him pass and he began the long walk home.

That afternoon he tore down the front of the house with the hammer and the ax and his bare hands. He set aside the broken door and the few loose boards already scattered inside the now faceless house. He dug a pit with the shovel and built a fire and he pitched those planks ruined or rotting into the fire to burn out the nails. By evening he'd climbed onto the precarious roof and pulled up all the cypress shakes and dismantled the rafters. He ate a light meal of rice and beans then carried on by firelight, pulling down the crosstimbers from the ceiling before he quit to stack the lumber he'd salvaged. He slept outside by the embers.

In the morning, he filled the bucket with marshwater and

wet his hands and rooted in the ashes to collect the nails, dropping them to cool in the water and periodically plunging in his steaming hands as well. When he'd got what he could he dumped the bucket and set out the nails to dry, and he recommenced the demolition of his house. By dinner he'd shelled all the outer walls, the caked bousillage infill decrepit and foul with rot. After he'd eaten, he kicked out the bousillage, knocking out the clots overhead with the butt of the ax so it fell over his head and shoulders in chunks. Then he set to disassembling the timber frame.

On the third day he pulled apart the flooring and arranged everything in piles around his plot and surveyed the supplies, planning the reconstruction with a stick in the dirt and taking mental inventory of what he'd yet need. He took the ax and the empty sack and hiked out toward the lake to foray the steamy rim, climbing over cypress knees and mucking through the mud up his calves, until he found a felled cypress trunk draped with heavy ferns and Spanish moss. He collected the moss and packed it into the sack, then he hacked away a section of the trunk and heaved and rolled it until he'd got it onto the nearest patch of dry land he could find. He sat it like a bench and panted in the dense humidity, took off his shirt and mopped his brow with it. He sat like that for ten minutes, his heart rate subsiding. The waters seemed to breathe, a feral breath putrid like a rabid dog's.

As noon came, he ventured into the surrounding trees and collected more moss, stuffing the sack til it bulged almost spherical though it weighed next to nothing. He ate some dry flatbread he'd attempted, powdery and tasteless, full of grit and so desirous of some moisture to make it even chewable that it desiccated his tongue and he had to dip his hands to lap the water there, what few sips of it he could stomach. He foraged for mushrooms but found none and finally gave up and set to the log. With the ax he hacked several pillars a foot square and about two feet long, each tapered at one end. These he stacked aside and then he returned to the trunk and cut another length. As night fell and the bayou began to move, the air itself constricting around him, he slung the ax on his shoulder and clung to the sack of moss with his arm wide, almost perpendicular to his torso, and he hiked home for supper.

As the sun rose the next day he took his ax and hammer into the marsh toward a distant neighbor's house. The man who'd owned it had been conscripted with Buford and Remy and he'd sent his mother, his two sisters and his young brother north to live with a cousin in Rapides Parish, though Buford knew from the reports he'd got in camp that the whole area had long been over-run after the fall of Fort DeRussy and what became of the family he never knew. Buford remembered the young boy weeping angry tears and throwing apples at his brother's head, the boy's face purple as he cussed the conscriptionists for not taking him as well. The boy's dog barking and running tight circles around the cart wheels. The boy's name was Charles, Buford remembered, and he cussed so well the conscriptionists nearly brought him along just for the company, but then the elder brother, Lambert Tasse, stole a pistol and held it against his own temple, knowing the conscriptionists were paid by the men they brought in. They let the cart go with the screaming boy inside while the sisters wept and the mother watched with flat blue eyes like bleached seashells. They shackled Tasse's ankles and five weeks later Buford watched Tasse's left shin disappear in a cannonshot. As several screaming men ran to help him, Tasse held his bloody stump in one hand while with his other he pulled his pistol and pressed it to his head the same as he'd done at his house. And this time he'd pulled the trigger.

Buford heard a noise in the reeds and he reached for a pistol he didn't carry but the ax came up in his fist and he gripped it tighter. A small dog, black where the mange hadn't taken the fur, emerged from the tall grasses and sniffed at him. They stopped in the trail and regarded each other. Buford squatted and set aside his tools and clapped his hands between his knees. Scout? That you? The dog whined and lowered its nose to the ground, stretched its paws forward. Your people moved on how long back, chien? Lord, it's a wonder you's alive. Buford moved toward the dog but it leapt backward and ran off into the marsh. He stood and watched after it but it was gone.

When he neared the old home he caught a scent he'd hoped to forget. His knees shook and he knelt in the loam, one hand on the hammer and the other tight around the broadax. Flies buzzed, in his head or in the marsh he couldn't tell. He shook his head, pressed knuckles against his temples. From where he knelt he couldn't see any house remaining, just a set of steps and two dry cypress blocks and a pile of flat stones where the hearth had been. But in the back of the property, down by the water, he spied what once might have been the separate kitchen if it still stood. In its place a pile of plaster and rotted lumber and a cloud of flies. He raised his shirtfront over his nose and crept up on it. With the broadax turned around and the haft as a lever he pushed into the rubble until a swarm of beetles spread from a gap and he fell away from them. Then he stood over the plaster and wood and swung the axe sideways like a scythe and flung away a great chunk of the debris, including a leathery black forearm and a piece of jaw. Buford retched and bent double and wiped his mouth on his arm. But he made himself look. A tangle of bodies inside, the uppermost desiccated but a few swollen limbs farther down, all black with decay though what color they'd been in life he couldn't tell. Squatters dead a week or more, no clue what killed them. Buford looked over the homestead, watched the grasses waving in the warm breeze. No sign anyone but him had been here for days. He backed away and sat on the houseless steps, tapped the peen of the hammer on the planks there for several minutes but decided the boards were useless. He looked to the collapsed kitchen now a mausoleum and wondered what to do about it. Finally he walked to the pile and kicked at the plaster several times until he'd flipped a section of it back over the bodies. He turned back toward his own home with his eyes on his feet and the ax and hammer heavy in his hands.

He tried a breakfast of dry bread but couldn't stomach it, so he spent the morning nailing a few of his own planks together and boring holes in the ends through which he tied a length of rope for a sled. He returned to the cypress trunk dragging the sled behind him. He collected more moss then finished the log, and he stacked a dozen cypress pillars onto the sled and tossed on the sack and he headed home, floating the sled down streams and across narrow pools whenever he could. At home he paced off his longest timbers and arranged a rough frame of cypress pillars every few paces. He laid the rails across the pillars and began to construct a new foundation. By evening he had the frame finished and worked into the night by firelight, squaring the frame and rearranging the interior pillars as he needed and finally laying down flooring. He slept that night on the open deck.

When he opened his eyes he was back in the smoking earth, mist and cannonfire commingling low over the torn dirt, and his ears were muffled, in sleep or concussion he couldn't tell. He raised up on his elbows and scanned the disfigured ground around him. Shallow rims of earth on all sides. He rolled onto his bare feet and crept over the lips of earth, each of which surrounded a wide pit. One pit held the tangled severed legs of men, blood caked over kneecaps or shredded thigh muscle. Another pit held a confusion of forearms and hands. They were the graves of amputations—he'd seen them in the field, behind the surgical tent where the screams echoed long after their issuing mouths had closed unconscious. Soon, he knew, a pair of privates or niggers would come with shovels and begin to fill the pits. He imagined the Judgment Day to come when all the wretched people of the earth would be resurrected and healed by Jesus, and he could see the limbs in the pits twitch and writhe, crawling forth on fingers like worms seeking out their reborn bodies. How would Jesus ever find them all? He wished instead for a barrel of pitch and a match. He staggered on, feeling drunk though he didn't remember drinking, between the two pits and toward the third, where he found a hundred severed heads, hair knotted together in pastes of blood and soil, mouths gaping at him. One of the heads was of his commander, Lieutenant Whelan, reddish-blonde hair on a high forehead and a white scar bisecting one eyebrow and a chin like a spade on a playing card. When he recognized the head, it moved, shoulders emerging from the heads around it and then the gory naked chest, a tarnished coin medal on a green ribbon pinned directly through

49

his flesh, and then Whelan raised his sword in his fist from within the heads and he began to howl.

When Buford woke he was scrabbling backward over the bare floor of his shack and he pitched shoulders-first off the platform into the grass. His fingers filled with loam and roots, and the pale dawn shuddered with his screams. He pawed his way to the nearest shallow pool and pushed his face into the water, screamed submerged so bubbles burst against his ears. He inhaled the muck and choked and coughed and finally vomited into the grass. He caught his breath. He sat on his elbows gasping and studying his new floor. He raised his hands and framed the shape of his house to come, held the box of his fingers there above the floor until his breathing subsided.

By the end of the week Buford had the true walls framed and raised. No time in his agenda to cure the moss in the old ways so that weekend he mixed the moss with mud from the marsh and constituted a new batch of bousillage, which he packed between the studs before he skinned the walls in tongue-and-groove siding. Exhausted, he decided to ignore the traditional garçonnière in the attic and instead bent long green poles to a shallow barrel ribbing bowed over the ceiling, and he thatched the ribs with reeds. This he finished by the middle of the second week, and at night he slept indoors on the floor while by day he began constructing a few pieces of furniture: a sturdy chair, a bench for his small porch, two storage boxes. From the broken door a small table; for a new door he simply hung a swatch of canvas draped like a curtain and weighted with a pole. Four square posts and a frame woven with rope for his bed. He sewed a canvas tick and stuffed it with dry moss and reeds and laid his mattress across the ropes. Outside he knocked down the top half of the chimney and stacked the loose bricks to reform the hearth for an outdoor kitchen. With the remaining lumber he built a simple bridge over a rivulet in the marsh to a patch of earth a few dozen paces off, and there he dug a deep hole until he hit soggy mud and the water seeped in to pool there, and over the hole he built an outhouse.

When he finished he bundled some reeds into a crude broom and swept out the small shack and appraised it, tested its walls, sat on his porch bench, lay back on his mattress, and wondered what the girl would make of it all, if she would approve. That night he lay awake in bed and stared out the one window at the wide moon flatfaced and bright in the dark-blue sky, and he realized the past week since the dream of Whelan was the first he'd slept without fear for years. He slept again that night undisturbed save by a steamy dream of the girl, and when he woke he was smiling.

VII

The old woman stepped from the plank into the pond where they'd killed the cavalrymen and she waded then swam to the other side. There, the sodden weeds sucked at her feet, and whenever she came this way now she grew nervous, worried that the bodies from the first year of the war, which the women had sunk in the marsh before they began using the well, had not forgotten her transgressions and waited there in the murk to pull her down to their revenge. She swam a ways further with her knees bent high and her toes curled, her gaunt arms pulling hard on the water and the salty marsh lapping up her chin to her lips. When she could no longer dogpaddle she let down her feet into the soft bottom and mucked up through the weeds to crawl ashore on the sandy bank beyond. She jogged panting up the grassy ridge of the chenier and paused in the stiff breeze to catch her breath. After several minutes she high-stepped through the grasses between the windswept oaks, the long tangled branches leaning hard away from the Gulf as though reaching for some lover lost in the marsh. At the seaside lip of the ridge she stopped and gazed across the long grassy coast to the thin line of the Gulf beyond. Even from here the soft crash of surf was audible and she could smell the pungent piscine scent of the beach. She put up a hand to shade her eyes and scanned the flat line of the horizon til she found the light blot she was looking for on the rim, and she meandered out across the grasses toward it. For several long minutes there was only the salty marshwater sluicing her ankles and her own huffing breath to match the lick of surf, but after a while she climbed a shallow rise and walked it til she met the girl, standing at the lip of a tidal cove, tossing baited lines out into the water. The girl wore boy's breeches with the legs rolled up and a wide straw hat, her muslin dress tied up in a knot like a long shirt. Beside her a wood bucket clacked with a half dozen angry crabs scrabbling inside, seeking purchase enough in the soft wood to escape but never succeeding. The woman said nothing for a while, only watched and caught her breath. The girl's arm jerked slightly and she sorted among the lines in her fist until she found the one with tension and hauled it in, hand over hand, to collect the small crab that clung there.

It shouldn't be us out here, the woman said at last. Remy's father used to bring him when he was a boy, they'd stand out here for hours on hours and crab a whole week's worth of meals. Should be our Remy out here crabbing with a boy of your own, never us.

Remy's dead, the girl said.

You don't know that, we just got Buford's word for it and him that's a deserter could just as easily lie.

Why would he lie about a thing like that?

The old woman looked up at her, ran her eyes over the girl

as a man might.

You remember when you and Remy was first courting? I couldn't keep that boy at home.

We did run around a piece, it's true.

I was awful lonesome in those days I can tell you. My Alphonse dead just two years before, Remy off chasing after you night and day. She looked sidelong at the girl. You can tell me, was you two foolin around them days?

Mother!

Well, it never come to nothing if you was, I suppose. She sighed and faced the girl and pressed a hand against the girl's hard belly. Remy my only boy, my Alphonse too drunk to give me another. I do wish you'd got pregnant before them soldiers come and called Remy up.

I sometimes wish it too, though it'd just be another mouth now.

A sharp gust rocked them on their small ridge and they were awash in dueling cacaphonies, the rustling trees behind them on the chenier and the crashing Gulf in front of them. The girl reeled in another crab and dropped it clacking into the bucket. Out on the horizon, a bank of clouds arose in shades of indigo and steel, a feathery brush drifting down from the lip to the edge of the Gulf. The woman raised an arm and passed her hand over the horizon as though petting the clouds, trying to smooth them out.

You remember the year before the war, all them storms we had?

I remember. It was one of them storms brought my family here and another made me near an orphan.

I never would of thought they could be three hurricanes in

two months. Just poured on over us like the flood of Noah. God's own wrath, like we was being prejudged for what only He knew we was about to engage in. Did you know the first one hit on the very anniversary of that Last Island catastrophe in fifty-six? You wasn't here then, but Last Island is a story they was still telling, and then here come that trinity of storms. They must be a reason to it, that first hurricane hitting on the same day as its predecessor. Didn't hurt us much beyond all the wind and rain, but we'd no idea what was coming.

The girl reeled in a crab. She sorted the empty lines from her fist and handed them to the woman to coil and tie. She said, I don't know whether to thank God or curse Him that our ship come in to land ahead of that storm. I'm glad to of found and married Remy, but I lost so much. That ship beached right up here in these salty marshes and us unloaded by the storm into the water. She looked along the rim of the coast into the thin blue haze of the distant shore. It was an awful mess out there.

I was among them that came to help you, though I don't remember you. Alphonse and Remy, Buford too, they was out in the sugarhouse trying to save the cane, though it was fool's work, nigger's work. I suppose those boys must of gone into Leesburg later to get theyselves a drink, cause I don't imagine how else he could of first seen you. I didn't allow no drinking in those days, not in my house.

You still don't.

Not having any drink about ain't the same as not understanding the need for one. Times like these change a body's perspective.

A line tugged and the girl reeled in another crab, small as her fist but snapping its free claw at her so fiercely she had to bash it against the bucket to get it loose from the line.

Why was those three out in the sugarhouse anyway? You said ain't no one knew what was coming.

I meant we didn't know the magnitude of God's plans, but we sure knew it was something. Like when you was little and knew you'd got in trouble but your mama told you to wait til your paw-paw gets home, and then all that day you know he's coming but can't imagine in your child's head what he gonna do. The weather that summer, it'd been awful hot, the air so thick you'd think it was smoke, and sunrise and sundown alike was heavy with mist and blood-red in the coming or dying light. We knew for certain the sky was going to break open sooner or later. Then here come that cloud, one great one like God's own anvil waiting to fall on us. They was some strange light in that cloud, not like no lightning I ever saw, not just the blue or yellow flashes you see but all sorts of colors including colors I ain't even got words for, and utterly silent, no thunder ever to reach our ears. And then it just passed on. Weren't no wind nor rain, just a show of what we was in for. So we all knew something was coming.

The girl nodded her head. She said, I remember when it did come. I don't know if Remy was in town for a drink—now he's dead, I'd tell you if I did know. But he sure was a sight running loose in them streets, all that howling wind pulling his clothes but the rain trying to stick those clothes to him, and him just a skinny thing like to blew away. But here he come flailing in the street, straight as a man could walk in all that gale, and he just headed straight for our little boarding house like he knew I was in there. I confess I didn't pay him much mind at the time, scared as we all was from the winds in the boards, the shingles up on the boarding house roof clattering in a ruckus like I ain't never heard. Some of them shingles tore loose and it was lucky the wind never blowed one of them shingles down to knock his head clean off. Poor boy, he finally got himself through the door and pushed it shut against the howling wind, and he still wasn't safe—all those shingles loose and the rain coming hard as it was, it was raining indoors as well.

I know it, the woman said. She raised a hand to the girl's shoulder and rested it there. You know that weren't the storm we lost our house in, she said, but I thought at the time it would be, so I packed what I could and followed y'all into town lest I get swept away with the rest. But then here come the winds, pulling theyselves around and tearing off back the way they came, and the waters went with them back out to sea. It was the damnedest thing, and I can tell you we was all relieved. Not that they weren't no damage. We did lose our outhouse and part of our chimney, and I think that first storm is what set our old house loose and ready to float off like it finally did.

The girl hauled in the last of the lines, the bait stripped from two and a pitiful fish dead on the third. She pulled it loose and sniffed it then tossed it into the bucket as well. The iron line of clouds remained out over the rim of the Gulf but further clouds had mustered north of them and the sky was now a watery green, the air damp. A few thin drops fell icy on the girl's arms and the wind turned cold. She handed the lines to the woman who coiled them as the girl took up the bucket in her two small fists, and they walked together back through the trees toward the reedy saltmarsh where they lived.

It's a wonder my people ever stayed here long enough to get caught in them storms subsequent, the girl said. Weren't no drinking water that hadn't been turned brackish from the floodwater, and hardly a dry place to stay. We got letters off to my brothers up in the Carolinas though we'd not heard from either in many years. The boys had some falling out or other with my daddy, but surely they'd have taken us in. I think if our ship hadn't been ruined and travel by land both expensive and troublesome we probably wouldn't have stayed.

Then Remy couldn't have courted you, could he?

No ma'am, ours was a love tempestuous for sure.

The woman watched the sky as they walked, turning the loops of line in her fingers. She looked at the girl and a smirk bent her weathered face.

It weren't just the storms that sent Remy to you, you know, the woman said. Them hurricanes flattened out all the cane, and once prostrated in the muck they weren't no crop to tend. A few of them field owners had some machines but those machines was just as deranged as the land itself and the sugarhouses been wrecked besides, so they weren't much to do but bring out the niggers or let the land go wild, all those little rootlets digging into the dirt and ruining the sugars in the cane. A lot of them bigger sugar plantations had plenty of niggers, but the one what supplied our sugarhouse and mill, it was short on niggers and in the end it weren't no use. So Remy, he had nothing to do but come calling after you.

You saying Remy courted me out of boredom?

I's saying it was you or work, and you's a far sight prettier than a hot sugarhouse going to waste.

But the girl had fallen behind and was standing half-crouched in the high grass, the stiff wind tugging her unknotted dress tight across her back and ballooning it before her. The bucket swung on its rope handle. The woman backstepped beside her and followed her gaze. In the thin drizzle they spied a high knee and hollowed crotch of a leaning oak, and within the shadowed burrow glowed tiny eyes watching the women. The feral creatures frozen there on the chenier beheld each other for some time, and the brisk fall shower dampened the women until the girl shivered involuntarily.

It's just a couple of old wolves, the woman explained. Strange them bedding down already though, or even at all. I ain't seen a wolf in years now, maybe not since this war began. Must be coming to the close and these here animals know it's time to get back to breeding.

That ain't what I'm looking at, the girl said.

The woman peered closer but saw nothing in the spitting rain. She reached the girl's wide hat from her head and set it on her own and squinted her eyes under the brim until she made it out, an old worn shoe rotten and half-decimated with the slobber of the wolves. The old woman stepped forward once and shook her head then stood straight. Well I'll be damned. Just like a couple old dogs, found them a shoe to chew.

That there shoe has the scent of a man on it, Mother. What if they get a taste for it? Find them bodies out here in the marsh? The ones we ain't dumped in the well?

The woman pulled her shawl tight about her shoulders and held it in one thick-knuckled hand while with her other she tugged at the girl's arm. Come on, don't talk that balderdash. We put them in the well for a reason, girl, and them others— But she hushed as she envisioned again the pale decaying arms reaching up from the weeds in the marsh. We'll just make sure the rest go in the well no matter where we kill them. Now come on.

The small eyes flickered as they watched the women go, and the women were silent as they went.

The rain was falling stiff now, the droplets needle-thin and just as sharp in their chill. The sky went dimmer yet. The women were shivering as they ran the grassy plain for the wide marshwater that separated them from their hut. The old woman hesitated on the bank, dreading the water for the cold as much as for the bodies within. Then she cussed and set one liverspotted foot cringing into the water, then her other, and the girl followed after.

By the time they reached the hut, the rain had mixed with sleet like birdshot and they ran inside shivering and rubbing their arms. They got a fire going and stripped from their wet muslin dresses and pulled blankets around them and sat leaning into the fire and listened to the sleet patter on the thatch roof. Frigid drops trapped in the thatch seeped through and dripped over them or hissed into the fire and they felt for a while like prehistoric figures alone in a living cave, wild and silent without words or even sign language. Just their great cold eyes alit before the fire and their jaws set firm in the cold, the little muscles at the hinges clenched to keep their teeth from rattling.

Neither woman wanted to venture out for water, so they gripped in both hands a crab apiece and broke away the belly shells over the iron edge of a cookpot. They threw the briny innards back into the wood bucket with the other crabs still scrambling to escape, and they roasted the meat in the topshells over the open fire. They ate in silence. The sleet ceased but the rain came harder and for a time the girl sat with her back to the fire, sucking crab meat from the legs, staring at the door as it rocked in the wind.

When they'd cleaned the shells and stowed them in a covered bowl in the corner, to pitch into the marsh whenever the rain concluded, they both stretched out on the platform bed and tried to sleep, but neither could.

You think Buford's all right in this weather? the girl said.

Sure he's fine. Don't you worry about him.

We ain't seen him in weeks now. Maybe he run off.

I hope he did.

I do hope he's all right.

You best hope your husband ain't truly dead, though if my Remy were to come back and hear you talking of Buford I don't know what he'd do.

I'm just concerned.

You keep your concern where it belongs. Married women who think after other men invite all manner of evil. You seen them wolves today. Maybe they was some rougarou keeping an eye out for a wayward girl.

You mean them wolf stories?

Way my mama used to tell me, a girl what lusts after a man falls prey to the forces of darkness. The rougarou ain't just a wolf-man but a punishment sent by God to ravage a girl in the night, and if she survives she becomes one herself.

That ain't the stories.

You grow up with the stories? I tell you true, you give in to wild nature wild nature will come for you.

Hush, Mother, I already can't sleep.

Well that's something to think on while you lie awake. Now let me be.

As afternoon fell into night the rain tapered off and the old woman snored, but the girl crept up from the bed and tiptoed around to the door. She slipped it open and peered into the night, trying to see into the rushes and make out whatever figures she might. But the moon, nearly full, slung wide and yellow over the rustling marsh and it spooked her. She swore for a moment she heard a howl in the night, and she scurried back to the bed and burrowed in the blankets and pinched shut her eyes. She murmured Remy Remy Remy in a quiet, deranged mantra and tried feverishly to call up his visage in her mind. But she never managed any vision but a horrid transfiguration of Buford's leering grin distended with jagged eyeteeth and his eyes yellow as the moon.

VIII

One cool morning in the damp fall, the girl rose early and pulled a wrapper dress over her cotton shift and, leaving it unbelted, stepped outside with a pail for water. She paused in the small clearing and gazed through the silvery light into the reeds as she had each morning and evening for weeks, but she saw nothing there. She sighed and ducked down the narrow path to the marsh pond. The water was cold as it swept into her dipped bucket but the sun was burning a mist out over the saltmarsh and soon it would be warm enough for chores. She hefted the pail and turned back toward the hut, and she saw him. He was standing on a slight rise of the reedbed with just his head poking up over the reeds. Then his hand emerged as though from underwater and he waved languidly at her. She watched him for several seconds, then she shook her head and started back up the path.

He paced her on some parallel path of his own making, toeing up now and then to peek at her over the tops of the reeds.

She walked on and tried to ignore him, though whenever his head jutted high enough for her to see, she glanced involuntarily in his direction and he smiled at her. When she came off the path into the clearing of her hut, she stopped and looked back to find him several paces away on his own path, shrouded in reeds. He had his hand cupped and was sweeping it toward himself. She wrinkled her brow and stared at him a moment before she realized he was motioning her toward him. She watched him swing his arm, and again. Then his head jerked and he dropped his hand, and the girl turned and saw the old woman emerging from behind the hut. She was carrying a bundle of sticks and a hatchet and she stopped to watch Buford. The girl ducked into the hut with the pail of water. Buford smiled at the old woman and waved like a child, then he disappeared into the reed beds, the breeze in the reeds masking his departure.

The woman ducked sneering into the hut. That old cur is back, sniffing around. He see you?

He saw me. Just waved.

You wave back?

My hands was full. I got better things to do than wave at old Buford.

I's glad to hear it. The woman stacked the sticks before a stool and sat to break them into kindling, her scowl deepening with the snap of each limb, her weathered hands tight around her work.

In the evening Buford reclined outdoors beside his cook fire, watching the stars watch him back. He looked among them to find a constellation in the shape of the girl's figure but he found none.

He said her name aloud in the night and he liked the sound of it. He looked to his house, the reused wood siding pocked with nailholes and ashen in the firelight, and he wondered what Clovis might take for some whitewash or if he could even find any. He pictured the firelight on white walls, then he pictured the girl against it, her red hair catching gold out of the flames, and he imagined her walking from the house to join him by the fire. He reached in his trousers and pulled at himself til he was hard, then he turned on his side with his trousers around his hips and he lay that way til he spent in the grass. He hoisted his trousers and sat upright to catch his breath, then he withdrew his pipe and loaded it with his last plug and leaned to the fire for a stick. A prairie lizard sprawled on one of the firebricks and it twitched its head toward Buford's motionless hand. They studied each other a long minute. Then Buford reached for the lizard and it leapt away from him into the fire. Buford jumped to his knees and peered into the hearth to see the lizard burst into orange flame and writhe into a blackened curl on one burning log. He stared at the shape of the thing. He shook his head and laughed at it.

By the time the sun had cleared the oaks up on the chenier and the mist had dissipated, Buford was sweating. He jogged up the ridge and wandered through the trees awhile, panting and swinging his arms wildly. When he came to the wolf den he stopped, almost the same spot as the women only ten days earlier, and he watched the hole but it was black and seemed empty. He crept toward it, his knees bent and his heart leaping. He stopped several paces off and watched it a while more. He hollered toward it but nothing happened. Hey! he called. Hey, you two mating in there?

No reply. He laughed and waved a dismissive hand, said, It's too early anyways. He stood and turned but then he stooped again and looked deep into the hole. It ain't too early for me, he shouted. You hear me? He faced out toward the reed beds and cupped his hands to his mouth. I need me a goddamn woman! A flock of speckled thrashers erupted from a clump of sage and spread across the sky, and he watched them away. He grunted, then laughed and tore off down toward the beach, splashing through the salty tidal waters and then pounding against the grassy sand in a gallop. When he reached the shore he splashed in the surf with abandon, his energy boundless. He stripped off his shirt and flung himself bare-chested into the waves and crashed against them as though challenging them to drown him. He won and won again. After a long while, as the tide receded and the sun hung out over the saltmarsh high as it would climb in the fall, he collapsed in the sand and napped there.

In the afternoon, the girl emerged sluggish as in a daydream and carried the pail again down the path to the pond. When she'd filled it, she looked up toward the reeds expecting to see him there but he wasn't. Even the wind was still. She waited a few moments—unsure what she waited for—then she rubbed her temples and dipped a hand in the bucket and ran it dripping through her hair. She started up the narrow path, the reed-heads bushy and brushing her cheeks as she went.

Halfway up the path the reeds rustled and Buford materialized from them as though created there on that spot whole and for the first time. She stopped short but said nothing, looked at him. He grinned at her, silent as well.

They stood like that.

Finally, he spoke: Come on up to my place.

She stepped sideways to slip around him, but he backed up with her and stayed in her sight.

I fixed it up. Just for you. Got a new bed and everthing.

I'm married.

Not anymore you ain't.

Well then I'm in mourning.

The hell you is. You barely knowed Remy, only went with him because they wasn't no one else after your parents died.

There was you, and I didn't go with you.

Remy saw you first, I saw you second. That's how it is among friends. But Remy, he gone, and now I's here.

Let me pass, Buford, I got things to do.

You got things to do indeed. But you look tired. That bed I made is real nice sleeping.

She feinted left then slid around him on the right and he pivoted to watch her go. The pail knocked against her thigh as she went, the water sloshing down her leg in little runnels. He ran his tongue over his lower lip then bit it.

I'll be waiting tonight, he called after her. Leave a lantern on the porch for you. You come look for it.

After supper, the women fell to the bed but the girl lay awake long hours into the night. She thought about Remy and Buford together. That first day when he'd burst into the boarding house wet and breathless from the hurricane, he looked like some prizefighter fresh from a victorious bout. He spied her among the huddled refugees, and as he made his way to the bar he stepped on several feet and shouldered one poor boy aside because he held his eyes on her, kept apologizing for his clumsiness but he seemed to be apologizing to her. When he ordered a whiskey and took up the little glass at the bar, he raised it to her and threw it back, then coughed into his arm from the power of it. The barman laughed at him.

Three days later and the storm long subsided, she met Buford coming into the boarding house. He'd been helping townsfolk repair the damage and at the end of the day he'd come to spend their proffered recompense on whiskey. She was in the parlor watching the people come and go, no other entertainment to be found. He brought two drinks to the cluster of chairs where she sat and he sat beside her, but at that moment Remy sauntered in, washed so recently his hair was still wet, and he sidled up to the chairs to greet her. He looked between them in surprise and then showed Buford a loopy grin and clapped him on the shoulder like he was on stage and she an audience sitting far in the back rows.

Buford, he'd said, I weren't aware you knew such fine ladies.

I don't yet have the pleasure, I's just about to meet her.

Well then let's meet her together—is that whiskey for me?

Buford looked at his two hands rising then falling in countermeasure as though weighing the drinks against each other, and then he said, Well, I suppose it must be, and he handed one up to Remy.

Ma'am, Remy said to the girl, my name's Remy Broussard, and this here's Buford Mire. And I for one is mighty pleased to be raising my glass again in your honor.

They talked only briefly, Remy chattering on excitedly and Buford quiet and watchful, sometimes of Remy but mostly of her. When her father arrived from outdoors and her mother descended from her room, Remy had put himself forward to meet them, and Buford had hung behind.

Her parents dead a month later, her father in the last of the hurricanes as he came in on a wagon he'd procured and then sunk in the bayou where he'd drowned, and her mother shortly after from the pneumonia she'd caught while looking for him. The girl adrift in the town and soon to be evicted from the boarding house, and Remy coming in with a fistful of wildflowers. She'd flung herself upon him, glad for some option at least. Buford there always in the background, watching. Always watching her, she realized now.

Awake still, she watched the old woman, listened to her snore late in the night. The breaths even and deep. Eventually she rolled off the low bed and crept out of the hut into the chilly starlit night. Still barefoot in her shift, she walked the marsh for an hour, restless, the shuffling of the reeds in the breeze the only constant sound, all the frogs and insects long migrated or deep in slumber though occasionally she heard the shrill, distant cry of an owl. Once, she thought, a dog yipped, but it might have been some other animal she didn't recognize. As she walked her agitation increased, and after a time she was running through the reeds, her breath hot in her throat and steaming into the cool night air, a feral passion sweeping over her. She hiked her shift to the tops of her thighs the better to run and when she came to a pond in the marsh she plunged in without breaking stride, splashed through the water cold about her calves but she so hot she barely noticed, her thighs pale blue in the starlight.

When she reached Buford's house she stopped and caught her breath. She stood in the dark curtain of reeds to study it, the rectangle shack small but sturdy, a drift of smoke from somewhere behind it, the lantern glowing soft gold on its nail by the canvas door. She slipped forward in the darkness and lurked on the porch in the lantern light, thinking to find a window to peek through but changing her mind. She searched the ground for stones but found none, then she crept around back and found the brick hearth there smoldering with the remains of Buford's dinner fire. She stole a brick from the lip of the hearth and she sneaked back into the reeds to hide. She studied the distance then chucked the brick at the house and it clattered on the porch. She ducked in the reeds and hid. Buford barged out shirtless with a pistol in one hand and a knife in the other.

Who's out they? He aimed the pistol into the dark, searching, then he spied the brick lying on the porch, and he toed it over the edge. He looked at the lantern hanging outside the door and he turned again to stare into the marsh, grinning. He stepped off the porch into the night, passing the pistol before him in an arc, until he came close to where she crouched. He sniffed the wind like a dog. He aimed the pistol into the weeds near her head and declared, I got you now, you's gonna die.

She squealed. Don't shoot, it's me! and he laughed at her.

I thought it might be. Get on up out of they and come warm youself inside.

The girl stood and slid around him and headed toward the house, but he caught her arm as she passed and he wheeled her around, seized and kissed her hard on the mouth with one hand clutching for her breast—she reeled back and slapped him smart, then shoved him wheeling backward. When he righted himself and came again, she punched him, her knuckles sharp against his cheekbone. He stumbled and scowled at her, his hand cupped over his cheek, then his face steeled and he clenched his fists and made for her but she was already leaving, and as he stormed after a few paces he laughed at her. She whirled on him and hit him again, a fist to his temple though he ducked away and she only clipped him, and then she raged back into the marsh.

He'd stopped laughing but held an unsure smile frozen on his face. Hold on, now, don't go, he called after her. I thought that's why you come.

She vanished into the marsh without saying anything, the only mark of her regress the occasional splash in a pool.

The next day he found her at the pond again, dipping her pail as every morning. He stopped her in the path between the marsh and her hut, and she sneered at him.

You get the hell out of my way.

I just want to talk to you.

I know what you want and you can't get it thisaway. I could kill you same as I killed others.

He fought against smiling at her, tried to look serious though he just wound up looking grim and unhinged. I know you could, he said. I didn't mean to offend you, I just figured it's why you come over last night.

Maybe it was, but a girl likes to be wooed, Buford. She pushed around him but he followed.

Well come on over tonight and I'll woo you.

She looked back at him but didn't break stride.

I'll do whatever I've a mind to, I don't need you ordering me around. Now you get on and leave me be.

Inside the hut, she dropped the bucket so the water slipped over the rim to seep into the earthen floor. The woman glanced sideways but kept at her work sharpening a long kitchen knife. You took you a while, she said while the girl reached into the rag-bin to wipe her brow.

Thought I saw a gator, the girl said. Just a hump of old tree, but I didn't want to risk it, so I stood still a while.

Too bad it weren't one. Gator's good eating and would set us up for a week.

I reckon they ain't no more trouble to kill than a man, but I don't know as I'd like to find out.

Shoot, they just like a man. Get a hold on they mouths and they can't do nothing to fight you off. The woman tested the edge of the knife and wrapped it in an oilcloth to set aside. My Alphonse used to wrestle gators out the yard ever morning just so's little Remy could go outside for his chores. They was one morning I woke to Remy shaking in his sheets and Alphonse stalking the house with a lit candle in one hand and that they knife in the other. She pointed to the oilcloth. Took me a minute but then I heard it, this shuffle and knock on the floorboards but no one up save Alphonse and him barefoot and tiptoeing. Thought for sure it was a ghost ambling about the house. After a while Alphonse went out to the porch and peered his head under the floorboards, like to break his chinbone on the wood coming back upright he jumped so fast. They was a gator right under the house. And Alphonse, he went right on under they after it. Bravest man I ever saw, but really, weren't no trouble if you knew how to handle them gators like he did.

I'm surprised Remy was so scared, the girl said. He seemed

about as fearless a man as I know of, and I seen him chase after a gator or two myself before he got called up.

The old woman laughed. That boy was his pawpaw to a tee, looked up to him with a mighty pride. Wanted so badly to be like his pawpaw that he took to wrestling blacksnakes just for practice. Ever day came in smelling to high heaven.

I sure would like to of seen that.

I wish you could see him still, the woman said.

That night the girl lay awake again, this time envisioning Remy, full grown and shirtless in the heat of day, grappling with long coils of serpents thick as his muscled arms, black as his hair. Alligators hissing and snapping around him like an audience. The sweat down his back. The black snakes gone pale, her own arms and legs now, his hands on her back, his chest hard and hot against her breasts. The visage before her not quite Remy's anymore, cast in shadow that she mistook for stubble until it spread over his whole face and the breath on her neck was someone else's. She wasn't thinking of Buford, but he was the nearest thing she had, and in the end she knew she needed him, or something like him. She rose carefully and sneaked across the bayou again, and when she came to his shack she didn't even knock at his doorframe. She just slipped in. His torso jumped from his mattress like a spring trap and he sat panting with a knife flashing in his hand, but when he saw her he set it aside gently on the floor and he stood and smoothed his hair, straightened the creases in his nightshirt.

I'm right glad to see you, ma'am.

Shut up, Buford. Then she kissed him. They soon fell to groping each other frantically, and as they kissed and groaned they collapsed on the floor, their knees and tailbones knocking on the wood, and they writhed there like fighting alligators. He began to pull at her shift but a thread popped, then another at the seam on the sleeve, and she pushed back his hand, her fingers in his. Careful, she said, her breath hot on his neck, and she reared to shuck her clothes as he peeled his shirt over his head and shimmied out of his drawers. They crawled onto the bed and fell into each other again, their mouths open and roaming everywhere, lips and tongues wetting each other's necks, chests, arms. He ran a hand around her breast and down the xylophone of her ribs to her hip, and she seized his small buttocks, her hard fingertips driving him toward her. His hand followed her hipbone around to her pubis and delved between her legs, hot and wiry nest moist and pulsing around his fingers as she gasped and clung to him, her thin arms like bars across his back. When he entered her they shouted together and then they were tearing into the mattress, their moans more like hollering, as though they each were lost in the marsh and in the darkness calling out for each other or God or both.

IX

On Christmas Day the women woke before dawn, the elder to piss in the marsh and the younger to unbury their two Sunday dresses wrapped in muslin and hidden in the bottom of a chest rarely disturbed. The girl shook out the dresses and hung them on a line outside the hut while the woman boiled water and brewed a bitter acorn coffee. They cracked a pair of questionable gull eggs into a pan, sifting the tiny bones and blood from the yolk as they could manage. After breakfast, the girl brought in the dresses and once clad helped the woman into hers, but the latter fought her the while. I's fed up with this nonsense, she said, don't see what the to-do is.

It's Christmas, the girl said. We already missed last Easter, I don't remember when we last attended confession.

And they's a reason for it, too, the woman said. I don't like Father Nathaniel much, seems he got funny ideas.

You ain't seemed to mind him two years ago.

Well hell. To tell it true, I can't face that priest knowing what we done. And nowadays, I can't bear to face the man what christened Remy knowing I let him die.

You might ease your conscience some if you let him hear your confession.

Father Nathaniel ain't got time enough in his whole life to hear a confession such as ours.

All right, fine. Maybe we just go to that Baptist church, then, ain't no one we know there and no priest to face. Get us right with God and we come on home.

But the woman was already undressing again, her usual wrapper dress within reach. Ain't gonna get no forgiveness from them Baptists. Besides, I already know about Jesus getting born. Like a pig in a pen just raised for the slaughter, same as our Remy, same as my Alphonse, same as all men.

The girl watched her for several minutes, but the woman changed into her wrapper dress and was already gathering traps.

I never saw the fuss in Christmas anyways. Was just a day at Mass and a family meal when I was a girl. Ain't nothing we got time for now.

The girl only shook her head, then she changed her dress and took up the pail to gather water at the pond. She stepped out the door to face a cold and quiet marsh, and she slipped indoors again for a shawl then walked barefoot and shivering to the small landing by the water. When she dunked the pail she heard a small splash and raised her head just in time to watch a blue heron fly wide-winged and dangle-legged out over the marsh, away from her. The sky was pink and her breath fogged in the air as she watched it go.

X

It was unseasonably warm that early in the spring and the woman had taken already to wearing the same loose, decrepit wrapper dress she'd worn in the summer previous, the hem wrinkled and near-ruined from her tying it up between her legs like pantaloons as she moved about the hut. The layers of underclothes she used to wear had gone to rag in the last few years, because she could little bear the touch of fabric anymore and preferred her wasted wrapper loose, untied by apron strings. But on this hot late morning, her home chores done and the real work still ahead, she had need of a belt, so she unhung a black leather belt with a tarnished Confederate buckle and cinched her dress at the waist. She took up a thin dagger and tucked it into the belt, then she tied an empty sack to the belt and picked up a bucket of rife fish heads she'd saved from a recent catch. Leaning on a stiff walking stick, she thrashed out across the reed bed away from the marsh, out into the sodden prairie fields to the stream where they'd set traps for crawfish.

The sun had risen high on its springtime arch by the time she reached the stream. She walked up one side, waded across the still-chilly water, and came down the other, tugging at lines and hauling up the wood traps alive with restless crawfish awaiting her arrival and their deliverance. At each trap she opened the slatted door in the top and reached out three or four crawfish. At her touch, the little crustaceans came alive like Napoleonic lobsters angry and plotting their escape. She slipped the crawfish clattering into the sack and shook the traps to empty them of previous, putrid detritus, then chucked in a few fresh fish heads and set the door and dropped each trap by turn back into the stream, aiming it on its line into the current. By the time she'd come down the backside of the creek and crossed again to return to the hut, it was near dinner time and the sack writhed on her hip with a score of crawfish. She was weary and kept her eyes on the ground to guide her steps as she drifted back toward the marsh, so the voice she heard startled her. She dropped the sack and her stick alike and whipped the long dagger from her belt and darted her eyes about to seek the source. She'd not even heard what words were spoken.

There was a man a few paces off with his hands in the air not in surrender but as though to soothe a dog. Whoa, he said, settle down ma'am, I just said howdy.

She scrutinized him closely, the way she might judge a hank of meat or a watermelon. He was tallish in a way though not abnormal, and his face was gentle and handsome, a scar here and there and a sharp chin but otherwise pleasant with a crooked smile breaking open his lips. His eyes glittered darkly. He wore gray trousers with a pistol in its holster and a clean Confederate coat unbuttoned and loose over a sweat-stained shirt, the gold embroidery at the jacket cuffs faded and worn, twin bars on his collar and a hand engraved medal hanging from the breast, a kepi hat squared neatly on his reddish-blond head. She held the dagger steady before her and pointed at the man.

Where you come from? she said. What you want?

I'm on leave, ma'am, just coming through on my way to Mississippi. I come from over the Sabine, up in Orange, Texas. I didn't want nothing but to say howdy.

She eyed him a moment longer then held him in her gaze as she bent and felt along the ground for her sack.

Well, she said, howdy back. Now get on with you.

She found the sack and with it tucked between her pinky and her palm she groped for the stick as well, the knife still clenched in her other hand.

You lost some crawdads there.

She flicked her eyes to the ground and saw three crawfish scuttling along toward a clump of grass. She shifted her crouch and leaned to snatch them and she looked up at the same time but the man was gone. She stood suddenly, a crick in one knee and her stance wobbly, and she pivoted in place to find him walking casually out in the marsh, a pack she hadn't noticed riding squarely on his shoulders, a rifle barrel silhouetted on one shoulder. She studied his departure. She wondered if she ran after him, tried her wiles on him as distraction, she might at some point gently slit his throat, but his pace was brisk for all the ease of his stride and he was long out in the marsh already. And when she thought on him, her skin shrank and her spine went cold, and she decided she was well shut of him, however much the goods on his back might have brought. She watched him a moment longer, then scanned the ground and found the three stray crawfish some feet away, scooped them into the sack and collected her stick. She walked after the man, the knife still in her fist.

She'd got another dozen yards and was reentering the marsh when she realized she still followed the man and that he seemed headed the same direction as she. She bent into a jog to regain some ground between them, but his gait was loping and long and he outstrode her easily. When he reached the reed bed, she called out to him over the whispering breeze. At first he seemed not to hear, but when she called again he slowed his pace. She began to catch him up and she called out a third time so he stopped and turned. He waited. The knife was still firm in her little claw of a hand.

They's a town just to the east, due east there. Leesburg. She paused and breathed hard, leaning on her stick. Place to sleep and eat you some supper. Up thataways. Can't miss it.

He smiled at her, his teeth yellow and sharp in the silver light of the afternoon sun.

I thank you, ma'am, but I reckon I'll just keep walking these here marshes, see what there is to see.

They ain't nothing to see, is what I'm telling you. All the homes is empty, everbody moved on into town when the men left.

Is that where you live, in the town? The smile was friendly but stiff on his face and hadn't broken yet, his lips upcurled even as he spoke.

The woman didn't know at first how to reply. She realized she'd not had a conversation with anyone but the girl and Clovis, and recently Buford, in almost three years, the only other people she'd bothered to meet the soldiers she killed in the marsh. She tensed her fingers around the knife haft but felt coldly alone out there on the edge of the reed beds, just her and this man who was himself almost not there, hollow somehow, ghostly. Without the girl armed beside her, she knew not what to do.

Well? the man said.

I's sorry, I don't mean to seem unneighborly. I just don't know how much I ought to reveal to a strange man concerning my living situations.

He dropped his head almost in a bow. I understand, he told her. How much can you tell me about the situations of others? There anyone else out here in these marshes? Anyone else passing through?

I keep myself to myself, sir, and don't bother none others. But like I said, everbody is up in Leesburg, ain't nothing really for no one out in these marshes.

He considered her, his hip cocked against the weight of his pack and his eyebrows high. He seemed almost to be smelling the wind for some scent of her intentions, as though he could sniff the truth from her. That creatural grin spread wider on his face.

So Leesburg it is, then. I thank you ma'am. He turned to go and she was glad to let him but an idea seized her and before she'd had time to consider it she blurted out for him to wait. He turned back to her.

You don't mind my saying, and I ain't judging nothing, but we ain't seen many men through these parts in some months whether in or out of uniform. You carry any news of the war?

His face went stony. Ma'am, that war's about as fought as it's going to get. There'll likely be a piece of fighting left on both sides, but I can tell you from my own observations that it's all but over. Truth be told, it's why I'm passing through these parts. I'm getting while the getting's good.

Did we win it?

Ma'am, I haven't thought it likely that either side would win for some time now. It's just been fighting for fighting's sake and both sides was losing. I don't reckon the outcome to be any different. All that's left now is unfinished business.

Well, she said.

Indeed. And he turned and walked out eastward toward town. She watched him off to be sure he was leaving, and at last she slipped the knife back in her belt and unpeeled her cramped fingers from the haft. She set down the sack and leaned the stick on her shoulder so she could massage the pad of her palm, then she shook out her hand and took up her sack and stick and she walked home.

When she arrived, she slipped in the rear of the hut and set down the sack of crawfish and went to the rain barrel for a ladleful of water. She called for the girl but got no reply. The water bucket and the washboard were gone, so she headed down the path to the pond. There she found the bucket sitting at the end of the plank and the washboard leaning against it. No girl in sight. She surveyed the reeds, the hot wind blowing swift. A new-broken trail barely visible in the reeds, cutting off in some other direction they'd never gone. A dread tightened in her gut and she flexed her fingers to ready them again for the knife. She listened for sounds of fighting, for cries or the breaking of reeds, though she heard none but the wind rustling the grasses and stirring the wide surface of the marsh pond. She searched the ground for signs, feet skidded in the loam or blood in the grass, but found none. She ran back to the hut and retrieved the old musket with its bayonet fixed and she returned, crouched, hunting. But she neither saw nor heard any indications of the girl or her fate. She ventured near the new trail and probed it with the bayonet but thought better of exploring it. She stood and considered the man off up the marsh, but he was headed east with no way to track back to this spot before the woman arrived. Where else for the girl to have gotten, who else to have accosted her? And then she realized, envisioned suddenly the wrestling bodies, the desperate grunts, almost could hear them. She scowled at the reeds. She muttered Buford's name aloud and thrashed back to the hut.

She pushed through the front door and threw the musket onto the bed as she marched straight through the back to the rain barrel and shouldered it at stride. Water coursed over the far lip then spilled in a torrent over her shoulders and back as her thighs strained against the weight of the barrel. She twisted her shoulder and managed to shift the barrel a few inches to the left, and with every rock of the water to and fro she managed another inch and another, until she'd revealed a now-muddy hole in the earth the width of the stovepipe that lined it. She sat on the ground and pulled from the stovepipe a cloth-wrapped squat bottle, the neck uncovered so the daylight shone in the thick green glass. Uncorked it. Held it tight against her bosom and lowered her nose to the mouth. Two inches or so of bright corn liquor swirled and flashed in the bottle, and the fumes made her dizzy. But about the mouth of the bottle, with the cloth at the neck tight in her fist, there lingered a faint aroma of sweat and spittle. Whether it truly lived there or was a fabrication of her mind she didn't care. The scent of her husband's lips and hard, sweet bite of the liquor left her swooning, her heart fast in her ribs and her fingers tight on the bottle. She rocked in the dirt.

In the fourth year of their marriage, when she still was young and their small house had stood in the clearing, she'd discovered the bottle in a similar hole, also beneath the rain barrel, dug she knew not when. She'd never minded him drinking in town or even out in the fields but she'd had a drunk for a father and had overimbibed herself as a girl when she'd got into her father's store, so she would not abide liquor in her house. When she'd discovered her husband's cache she thought to smash the bottle against the house. But she realized she'd never seen the bottle before, meaning it had never been in her house. Alphonse in his quiet way had kept to her rule, and he'd hid it in a spot Remy would have to be strong as a man to discover. She respected that as he'd respected her, so she returned the bottle and left him his secrecy.

Remy never did find the bottle, and she herself had drunk from it only once, a thimbleful on the day Alphonse had died in the field. When a hurricane blew through the first year of the war and destroyed their house, she'd found the bottle still corked and clung to it, the last thing of her dead husband's she had left. She kept it from the girl, this memory hers alone, and she'd re-dug the hole and put the bottle in its proper place as her husband had left it.

She'd not breathed in near a minute and her breath caught in her chest. She would not allow her eyes to wet, and she corked the bottle and shoved it into the hole then wrestled the barrel back atop it. Returned indoors. Returned to her chores.

When the girl returned that afternoon the woman asked where she'd been.

The girl casual and bright, flushed in the face, thirsty from some labors the fruits of which were nowhere in the hut: I thought I saw that old wolf come up near the house. I thought to scare it off lest it try for us, so I went tearing into the reeds.

That a fact, the woman said.

Weren't nothing out there, but I walked on out to the chenier to check that old den anyway.

And?

I don't know. Didn't look no different that I could see, but I didn't see them wolves.

You best not be hunting anything youself, least of all any wolf. Never know if it's real or supernatural.

You mean them rougarou tales? That's your bedtime story, not mine.

Some bedtime stories is real. You best stay here with me.

I'll be fine, I know what I'm doing.

You don't know nothing. The woman thought to explain about the Confederate she'd met but kept it to herself, wary of revealing too much to the girl lest she need the information for some later tactic to keep the girl nearby.

XI

The next day Buford found the girl by the pond and he motioned for her from the new trail he'd tramped, but she hissed at him.

No, Buford, I can't.

What do you mean you can't? I done waited all winter for you, hell, my whole life, and I aim to catch up on lost time.

Mother is wise to something, she hissed. Not to us, but she's watching.

She ain't your mother.

The girl waved him off. Not during the day no more. I'll come again tonight.

You damn right you will. Then he slunk sullen back into the reeds.

That evening when the girl sneaked out the old woman's snores chased her into the night. The girl broke into Buford's house in a rush and slapped tight the canvas doorflap, hurried to the middle of the room and shucked her thin shift to stand naked over the bed.

Come on, let's do it quick, I got to get back.

Buford looked at her only a moment as though to protest but then he was up and out of his drawers in one motion and he grabbed her and threw her onto the mattress, then dove after.

Back in the hut the old woman snored with her eyes open. When the girl had gone the woman rose and took a knife from their collection and followed in the dim quarter-moonlight, the wind cold in the reeds. But even above the rustle she could hear the pants and huffs of the girl as she ran through the bayou. The old woman cursed silently and jogged after for a bit then simply stalked the girl fast and determined in the night, knowing without having to follow where they both were headed.

The old woman crept up on the shack in the thin light. There was a soft glow in the grass to the side and she slid that direction until she could see the faint lantern light through the glassless window. She sneaked up to the window and peered inside. There the two lay entwined naked on the bed. The girl was talking but she couldn't hear. The woman leaned back away from the window and slid to the ground and thought. Then she crawled like a dog around the side of the house to the porch and she pressed her ear near the thin canvas door. She heard murmuring and she plugged her outward ear with her finger to hear them talk.

I don't like coming over here at night, the girl said. The bayou is scary in the dark, all manner of things running wild out there.

You safe here.

It ain't here I'm worried about. There's gators and wolves out there, and what if some soldier or deserter like you was to wander into the bayou in the dark? He could come upon me without me knowing.

Don't be stupid. You killed how many men already with your own hands?

The girl laughed. You're right, it ain't them I'm worried about.

What then?

You'll think me foolish.

I think you foolish already.

Mother, Remy's mother, she talked once of the rougarou.

That old company of crazy boys?

What? No, I don't know what that is. I'm talking about the wolf-man what stalks wayward girls in the night.

Ain't just girls. They'll stalk anyone.

Stop it, I still have to walk back tonight.

It's all just stories, girl. Don't pay them no mind.

There was a long passage of silence during which the woman dared to pull aside the canvas door a sliver. She could see them in there, long and naked on the tick, orange in the lantern light. Buford raised an arm to scratch his wiry hair and the old woman flinched but stayed put, peeking through the door.

Still, he said, don't hurt to be cautious. You see one you just take your knife and cut him a good one, anywhere you can get him.

They're supernatural, you can't kill one.

Don't have to kill him, just draw you some blood and he'll change back to human and run off and leave you be. Can't tell no one about it though, not for a year at least. Not even me.

Can't tell no one?

You tell a soul or even God Hisself what you seen when the rougarou changes, or even that you met one, and a year ain't passed, you're liable to change to one youself.

Buford, damn it! Now you're walking me home, I ain't going alone.

Sure you are. Like I said, you a killer and kept that secret long enough, surely you can cut a old wolf-man once and keep that youself as well.

I can handle men just fine, it's animals and the supernatural what scares me.

I'm man and animal alike ever time you come to see me, and you handle me just fine.

He rolled over her and took after her again and she clawed at him in delight. The woman averted her eyes, fell backward off the porch and staggered into the brush. She wandered toward home blind and mute with fury, thinking of her son and superimposing his face over Buford's so she had to shake her head to clear the image of her son naked on the mattress with the girl. She thought of her own husband and herself naked in their own mattress, his strong lean arms on her, the thrust of him. She climbed up on the chenier and through the thin oak woods to the ridge and stared out over the marsh toward the Gulf, the long curling lines of the surf glinting in the small moonlight out in the distance. She squatted in the grasses then lay back and clutched at her muslin dress, the memory of her husband as hot in her mind as her hands between her legs, her fingers working through the thick gray hairs and her palms pressed hard together over her small bone, and as she pressed her thighs together over her hands she wept.

When she returned to the hut the girl was standing in the

doorway frozen and she screamed when the woman approached behind her.

Good Lord God, Mother, I thought you was a haunt.

I had to take care of some private business, of the more solid variety. I woke and you was gone.

I had similar business, the girl said. She looked toward the ground and rubbed her thigh absentmindedly.

Well, let's get us to bed then, you look tired.

They ducked inside and lay down on their pallet. The girl looking at the woman nervously. The woman eying the girl.

I think you was right about that wolf, the woman said. I think I seen it out in the beds while I was doing my business.

You seen a wolf out there?

Or something like a wolf. Bigger than. You best be careful, not venture too far from here. We'll do our toilet closer to home from now on.

XII

The crawfish traps all proving unproductive and the wild fruits still months from maturing and the women tired of crabbing, they took to venturing farther from the marsh, working their way systematically northwestward toward the old cane fields and the sugar mill where Remy and Alphonse and Buford had once worked. They came to the edge of the cane fields and stood a long moment in vigil over the flattened, fallow rows forgotten by men long gone. The woman breathed unevenly and the girl thought she might be in tears but the woman only spat in the earth and marched on.

By the end of the week they were waking earlier and wandering farther each day, and they came at length to an area the girl had never seen but that the woman seemed to recognize. Lordy, she said, have we come this far? She led the girl through a wide shallow pond, the women with their skirts untied and hoisted high on their thighs, and up a grassy rise to find the home of the woman's sister. The girl had heard of her and knew the home to be long abandoned, the woman's brother-in-law still away and the sister packed up to follow him from camp to camp. The girl had suggested they move into the home when their own had fallen in the storms of that second year in the war, but the woman would not hear of squatting in another's house, even her own sister's.

When they arrived at the home they found some family unknown to them had struck on the same idea and then abandoned the home again. What furniture remained the woman did not recognize, and in the kitchen they discovered the bones of a cat piled in a black knot of rotted skin and fur by the back door.

They scavenged the cupboards but found nothing left of any use. In the main room, they took down the two curtains and rolled them into a bundle. In the bedroom they found a rotted cloth doll, which the girl picked up a moment to smooth and straighten before placing gently on the floor in the corner, but they found nothing of any value. They ventured around back to see if the garden was still producing but found it planted with oxeye daisies, which had just begun to flower.

Well hell, the woman said, and she ripped a fistful of the daisies from their stems. No wonder they run off, didn't have sense enough to keep the garden. She tossed the flowers to the ground and circled the bed. The girl bent and ran a hand over the heads of the daisies. I just realized it's near Easter, she said.

Don't go talking about no church, I ain't interested.

Might be nice to hear a sermon, though.

You want a sermon? Jesus died and resurrected and then run off to Heaven to leave us sinners here. Amen. The woman squatted at the back of the garden to root among the rows for any onions or radishes that might have been overlooked in sowing the daisies.

Surely you believe he will return, though.

I keep waiting for him, but today don't look too likely. The woman scooted along the back of the garden, digging in the soil. I don't know that any as leave will ever come back. Then she looked up at the girl through the flowers. Not any's worth a damn.

The girl snapped a daisy from its stem and held it to her nose. These here are like them I wore in my wedding. You remember, Mother?

They ain't a damn root left back here, the woman said.

They did look pretty in my hair, set off that pink organdy shawl I wore over my wedding dress right nice. I swear I never saw Remy grin so big nor look so red in the face as he did there at the altar.

We'd as well head on back, the woman said. It's late, and I's tired. As they turned to round the house they found a stack of firewood spilling from the side of the house, and the woman took the bundle of drapes from the girl and unfurled them to make a sling. Come on, she said, help me load some this wood. Take us longer getting home but saves us the trouble of cutting our own.

They stacked the cut logs lengthwise in the drapes so they could take up a side each and carry the wood between them in the sling. Every few logs they would stop and heft the sling to test its weight.

The girl said, I'd like to wear flowers on my hair again.

The woman unbent from her labors and pointed the log in her fist at the girl and said, You'll never.

Oh, Mother, the girl said, but the woman interrupted her.

Never! You hear me? Next time you wear daisies in your hair

will be your funeral, so's you can go to meet your dead husband looking the same as the day he married you. But never before.

In the warm daylight the old woman walked through the marsh to Buford's house. She waded across the front pond and stepped across the flat grassy yard to his porch, knocked on the frame beside the canvas door. She paced the porch a few moments then pushed aside the door but found the house empty. She walked around the outside of the house, past the brick hearth and into the weeds until she found him out by the back pond, napping in the grass with one arm tossed over his eyes. She walked into the weeds to stand beside him and she kicked him awake. He grabbed her calf and grinned up at her shut-eyed but then he felt up along the calf, furrowed his brow, and he raised up to look at her, squinting in the sunlight.

Shit, it's just you. He yawned and lay back again.

You do like to sleep, don't you?

The sleeping man's net catches the biggest fish, vieille.

Some of us has work to do. We seen the cane fields a few days back and they's a sorry sight. I know it ain't a one-man job but they's all abandoned now, you could claim them for your own, get them ready for when we get some help or some niggers or both.

He yawned again. It's too nice to work, and won't be long before it's too damned hot.

And what if they's some soldiers coming?

He opened one eye to look at her, a sly perpetual wink.

What soldiers? We ain't seen nothing all winter long and ain't likely to again.

I seen someone just the other day, out in the prairie.

Buford sat up and looked at her, his arms behind him like the legs of a tripod.

Who? Who'd you see?

Just a man, looked like he lit out same as you. Seemed after something but said he was headed to Mississippi.

Buford smiled, flopped back into the grass and rolled away from her. When he spoke his voice came half muffled from the pit of his elbow.

You get anything good off him?

Didn't kill him, the woman said. It just him and me out they.

That's too bad. I'd of killed him.

He said the war's ending and soon you and me won't have nothing left but real work to do. We'll be like to starve.

I'll find some way to work. Ain't that many men left to come back, folks'll need men like me.

Folks need men now but never men like you. She squatted next to him and peered over his shoulder. He rolled onto his back to look at her. She said, We don't live same as most folk, you and me. We have our own ways.

He frowned at her and shaded his eyes to see her better.

Right now my way's sleeping, so might could you leave me to sleep in peace?

Maybe you don't want a peaceful sleep. Maybe you want to sleep with me.

Buford raised his head from the ground and laughed, a big blast of a guffaw.

Damn, woman, what I'd want to sleep with you for?

She stepped over his supine form, a leg on either side of his hips.

You a man, I's a woman. Don't take much more reason than that.

You's a old woman.

Shut your mouth. Take you a good look.

She hiked her skirt up about her thighs and flared them a moment then unstraddled him to squat beside his face. I ain't old inside, she said. She dipped a hand under her skirt and brought her fingers under his nose to trace his lips. Come on and try me.

He grinned at her, then he groaned and sat up, put a hand on one knee and hauled himself from the ground.

Oh, I think I'll just go have me a swim in the Gulf.

Buford, wait. She dodged around him and cut him off, wavering from foot to foot to intercept whichever path he might take. He grinned and cocked his hands onto his hips.

What do you want, woman?

She sneered at him. Don't play stupid to me, Buford, I ain't no girl. I know what you want and you know what I want.

He crossed his arms on his chest. Go on and explain it to me anyways. I'd like to hear you say it.

You and my daughter. I want you to quit her.

We's friendly is all. Ain't no harm in neighbors being friendly.

I seen you both with my own eyes. You taking advantage of that young girl.

He waved her off. She the one come over to me, he said.

After you asked her to.

He turned to walk back toward his house but she followed close behind him.

I asked her, I never made her. I's a man out here alone in these marshes, she's a woman. What you expect us to do?

She another man's wife, Buford.

He turned to face her.

She's a widow. Your son is dead.

The woman leaned up onto her toes to press her face closer to his. Her lips were thin and her forehead quivered, her jaw clenched.

God damn you, Buford, coming back here by youself, leaving my son out they in that Godforsaken war. Now you'd try and steal his wife, too? From your best friend?

I'd look after his wife, yes ma'am. Look, she ain't your daughter-in-law no more, she's her own woman. She needs a man. It's just the way of things.

It don't have to be. You could leave, go somewheres else.

Where else would I go? Besides, I deserted. If I leave the bayou someone'd find me. They'd find me and hang me. No ma'am, I's happy right where I is.

Then you leave that girl be.

He rested his hands one on each of the woman's shoulders. I'll make a deal with you, how's that? I'll marry her, make us honest in the eyes of God.

You got a hell of a nerve! She slapped away both hands and put her fists in his face. My poor Remy must be spinning in his grave.

Well at least you admit he's dead.

That's right I admit it, and now that girl's all I got left in the world. My Alphonse long dead, a good man but drinker enough to never give me but the one son and now my Remy gone, too. I need that girl. I can't live without her.

I didn't know you was so sentimental.

I can't kill without her. I tried, I'd of killed that man I met out in the marsh cept I couldn't handle him alone. I don't have her, I'll starve.

Maybe we'll take care of you, the two of us. One big happy family.

You wouldn't, you'd get her pregnant and that'd be the end of it, you'd shunt me off out of the way and leave me to die.

Damn but you have an imagination.

You can't marry her, Buford.

Alright, then, we'll just keep on being friends. Just friendly neighbors.

That ain't no good, she'll get pregnant anyways and she'll leave me.

I'll tell her not to leave you. And they's plenty of ways to stop a pregnancy.

He turned again to head to the house but she darted around him and pressed both hands on his naked chest. Buford, I'm begging you. When the war is over for good and things settle themselves back to normal I can round up some new niggers, old Lincoln's proclamation be damned, and I can get the sugarhouse running again, grow some cane of our own, rebuild the house and plant some garden and what all. But I got to have the means for doing it. I can't kill without that girl, I need her. Wait til we get us enough to get me started and you can have her then.

He sneered at her. You asking too much of me, old woman. Even if we win this war, they's no telling if or when you'd get you some niggers or ever get those damn fields running. You'll likely always have some reason or other to hang onto that girl. You just want her cause she was married to your son, and I understand that, he was a friend to me like a brother, near the only family I ever knew, and I miss him almost as much as you. But I need me a woman.

That's natural, Buford, it is. And you can have me. She unbuttoned the blouse of her dress and tugged the sleeves from her arms to let the blouse hang loose about her waist, her heavy breasts long on her gaunt chest. She threw a leg around him and rubbed her pubis against him. Come on, Buford, I know how to please a man. Have at me.

He turned his head away as though to avoid the tongue of an overeager hound. I ain't interested in you, he said.

She shoved away from him and dragged the sleeves back up her arms, left the dress unbuttoned. God damn you, Buford, you ruining me.

That ain't my concern.

You just remember you said that, Buford. She rebuttoned her top so angrily she misaligned the buttons to their holes.

Meaning?

Meaning I aim to make it your concern. I'll find me an army officer and report you out here. I'll burn down your shack. I'll stab you both in your sleep. You know what they say, Buford, that bones don't float.

You go on and do it, and you won't have her to help you kill anyways.

She slapped him and stormed back across his yard and into the reeds. He lurched after her a few steps, seething, then he shouted into the reeds, You damned old hag!

He paced his small land kicking up clods of dirt and grass, threw a loose brick into the back pond, hollered at the sky, then he stormed inside and sat at his table to drink from his jug. But instead he only held it, the clay neck cold in his fists.

Their first week in the war, the company still on the march to the camp where they would drill, the men had bivouacked near a large cane plantation and Remy and Buford had sneaked away in the night to walk the rows. It had always been their favorite pastime, hiking out to the fields near their sugarhouse and wandering between the stalks in the late evening. They kept a jug stashed out in the fields, a trick Remy had learned from his father, and they would take turns carrying it on their shoulders as they walked. Remy liked to break off a shoot of cane and chew it while they walked and drank. Buford never had the taste for sugar but Remy was enslaved to it. But this night, on the march and no jug to be had, they only walked, touching someone else's forgotten stalks ready to rot where they stood. It was then, just a week into the war for them both, Remy had first offered up the idea of deserting.

We ain't but just left, Buford had said. Don't say you scared already.

I ain't scared, I just don't like being gone. We didn't leave them with much, don't know how long we'll be away.

We'll be back in a month. Besides, your mama and your bride'll take good care of each other. The one's smart and the other's crafty, they'll be fine.

I had hoped to get her with child before we left.

Shoot, I should of told her you was slow. I'd of played madame with her myself if you hadn't tricked her into marrying you.

Careful, Buford.

I's joshing you, Remy, and you know it.

Nearly three years later they passed back through the same country, running in the dark with no time to touch the cane if it had still stood, their footfalls soft on the long-rotted stalks as they bent across the field toward whatever shelter they could find. Somewhere in the night behind them, the wolfish demon-man Lieutenant Whelan pursued. A night spent in an abandoned sugarhouse, Remy whispering in the dark: I tell you true, the first thing I'm doing, before I wash or eat or anything, is putting a child inside my wife.

You let me know if you need help, Buford had said.

Four days later Remy's head burst open.

Remy had given his friend a note two years before. He'd folded it into a tight square, the girl's name scrawled across the front in a shaky hand. I aim never to give her that, but just in case, you keep it on you. You promise me it'll find her.

On the day Remy died, Buford crawled through muck and fields never daring to raise his head, all his meager gear behind him save a knife in his belt and the letter in his pocket. In the night the moon was only quarter-full but the sky was clear, and in the faint starlight he unfolded the letter and read it.

My dearest love, if your reading this I must be dead. Greave not, for tho I is no longer able to return to your tender embrace, I am now at least beyond the horrors of this war. What awaits me in the Afterlife—a chorus of Angels or the flames of Hell—I do not know. If the flames of Hell, they will feel a cool releef from what I have seen and done. If a chorus of Angels, tho I do not deserve them because I fought only so you would never think me a coward and never had the stake in this war that other men had, they will seem as hollow as the echo of those stones we use to toss in that old well while making our wishes, for no Angel could ever sound to my ears as your voice does. In either place I will miss you, but know that whatever my destinashun, I am at peace. Be always friendly to Buford, who will look after you and Mama as a neighbor and a friend. Your loving husband, Remy.

Accompanying the note was a folded scrap of paper bearing a crude sketch of the girl's face, her features roughly outlined in charcoal but her narrow black eyes unmistakable, the tilt of her head and the shy smile hers alone. Buford read the letter twice, and once each day thereafter until the afternoon he found the priest whose cassock he'd stolen, when he'd left the letter in his uniform pocket as he changed his clothes.

XIII

That night after supper the girl and the woman lay side by side for a long time on the pallet, but neither breathed very heavily. The girl wasn't sure what to do. She kept rolling her eyes toward the woman to gauge the depth of her slumber but could make no guess in the silence. Finally she could wait no longer and she rose to sneak away. The old woman snorted once and turned her head but her eyes stayed shut; the girl crouched immobile in the middle of the hut and watched the woman, then after a few moments she crept on. When the girl opened the door the woman rolled over on the pallet and said, Where you going?

The girl froze and looked back.

I—I can't sleep. Thought I'd step out into the evening for a bit.

The old woman sat up and patted at her forehead with a cloth.

Yes Lord, it is humid these nights. Hard to sleep indeed. I think I'll join you.

They stepped out to the front of the hut, sat in the steamy night on a stump and an upturned bucket. The sky glowed an eerie shade of burnt ocher, a thick quilt of cloud slung low in the sky and the evening light unearthly over the marsh. The air soupy and astir with cricketsong. The old woman rubbed her neck and looked about.

Shoot, the air's so thick now they ain't no breeze.

No, the girl said.

They listened to the cricketsong a while, the girl staring seemingly into nothing but her gaze to the sky near the direction of Buford's house. The old woman watched her watching the reeds, and she thought of something to say. Finally she closed her eyes as if in memory and then looked at the girl.

I was dreaming earlier, the woman said. Dreamed Remy come back from the war.

The girl looked at her. You miss him something terrible, don't you.

Don't you?

Sure, Mother, I miss him.

You ain't never cried over him. I noticed. Ain't you sad your husband is dead?

The girl glowered at the woman, tightened her fingers over her bare knees.

I am sad, yes ma'am. But he ain't coming back. You and me learned enough about death these last few years to know there ain't no use in pining. They don't come back, they don't even hear you.

Not them bastards we take from the war, maybe. But our Remy's different. You don't think he's watching you now?

Suffering ain't a favor we do for the dead. If Remy was to see me now, he'd want the both of us to carry on without him. Remy knew I loved him while he was here and now he ain't and that's an end to it. Ain't no use in resting in the past nor leaning heavily onto grief.

The woman leaned on her stool to touch the girl's hand on her knee. The girl pulled it back and stared hard at the woman.

I's sorry, the woman said, I is. I didn't mean to accuse you of nothing. And I know you must be lonely, too. An old woman ain't no kind of company for a girl such as youself. She closed her eyes, then she opened them bright in the glow of the sky and she smiled at the girl.

I tell you what. I'll find you a good husband. Soon's this war is over I'll go on into Leesburg with you, we'll go to that boarding house again and we'll find you someone good to marry.

The girl looked hard at her then out across the reed bed, in the direction of Buford's house.

The woman continued undeterred.

When this war ends the men'll come back, not just the deserters and the ruffians but the officers, good men of some distinction. We'll find us such a one from among them and get the sugarhouse going again. We'll get us some niggers and start our own fields even.

I don't know nothing about no cane.

You'll learn, we'll find you a good sugar farmer and you'll learn.

The girl made to shake her head but it became a double-take as they heard reports out in the distance and they bolted upright, the bucket toppling over. A faint orange glow in the clouds and a black plume of smoke rising out to the west. Another explosion and the rapid pop of riflefire.

Damn, they's fighting out in the prairie!

The woman grabbed her by the arm, tugged her toward the hut.

We best get started that direction. We can't wait no more for them to come wandering in to us, we got to get closer.

They dashed inside and dressed quick and silent in the darkest clothes they had, the skirts tied up into short pants, then they grabbed all the weapons they could carry and rushed out into the night, racing stealthily through the rushes toward the ominous glow in the clouds. It took almost forty minutes near-sprinting to break free from the marsh and then they ran low and careful across the open prairie. The riflefire grew less frequent as they ran, but whenever they heard it they heard it louder, and soon they'd come as close as they dared, the fiery reflection from the clouds above them washing the prairie in a dim light almost like daybreak, the light the color of a fresh coal. They both knelt in the grass and scanned the prairie about, looking for a place to hide themselves as well as the likeliest spot to find the scattered troops.

The girl spied a ditch running low through the grass off to the south, and near it a stand of scrubbrush. They whispered in broken code and devised their plan, then the girl handed her cane spear to the woman and they separated. The woman slipped off toward the ditch where she lay prone with her chin in the dirt, hidden by the shadow of the tree, while the girl ran into the open prairie, loosening her skirts to fall about her legs as she scanned the flat horizon.

They waited several long minutes, maybe a quarter of an

hour. More reports, some close, some far off to the south near the beach. Then the girl spotted the brown silhouette of a man running frantic from the battle, his rifle loose and wild in his grip. She stood and looked toward the ditch then rushed to intercept the man. She waved her arms and the man came up short and raised his rifle but she called out to him, made sure her voice came high and sweet, and she rushed toward him so her skirts flew wide. He lowered the rifle and looked about him in the night. When she reached him she was panting and she said, Are you all right, is everything all right?

Ma'am you need to run out of here, there's a battle nearby and this is no place for a lady. His eyes frantic and his legs dancing, he was ready to bolt again, she could see it.

I got a place to hide, she said, over here over here, and she pressed against him so he didn't know how else to respond but to back away, and she managed to turn him and aim him toward the ditch. Run, she said, run to them trees you'll be safe there. He dashed off toward the trees just as she saw another shadow out in the prairie racing their direction. She pushed him into the ditch and the woman caught him on the end of the bayonet, his eyes wide and wet with surprise. She pitched him over into the deepest part of the shadows and hunkered down as the girl raced into the prairie to meet the second man.

Ma'am, get off this field, they's Yankees about!

I know, the girl said and she flew into his arms. I know thank God you're here, I just seen one run into them trees where my mama's hiding, hurry please and help her.

The woman set aside the musket and slipped up and into the clump of brush and waited. The Confederate dashed into the ditch and without warning aimed and fired into the body on the ground before seeing that he, too, was a Confederate. He looked about and then back out into the prairie where the girl was scanning the horizon again but she was the last he saw, the woman standing from the brush behind him to slit his throat, and he fell into the ditch beside his compatriot.

By the time day lit the clouds a fierce yellow and began to burn them away, the skirmishing had drifted north and back westward again, and the women had moved ditches twice, amassing in each three or four bodies for a total of ten dead soldiers. In their hurry to kill and move on they'd abandoned their usual stealth and four of the men they'd shot with pilfered pistols, one right out on the plain for all to see, though only the dead man saw it. When it was over, they thought of venturing west into the steaming battlefield itself to explore for abandoned bodies, but out on the prairie they felt exposed and unsafe, and they chose instead to strip what they could from the men they'd killed and leave it at that. They didn't even bother with the uniforms, just took the few packs from them that had one and stuffed them with firearms and knives and watches and coins and whatever else they could rummage quickly from the blood-soaked pockets, and then they ran as fast as they could manage back into the marsh.

It was midmorning already by the time they staggered into the reeds, and once they had some degree of safety, they changed course and headed south toward the chenier, up onto the shallow rise there and into a small grove of oaks. Here they collapsed, gasping and exhausted, and took turns sleeping away the rest of the morning in shifts. When they'd rested, they sat in the shade of the trees and rummaged in the packs. One man had carried a flask still half-full with some liquor, and another had a tin case with six cigarettes inside. They struck a match and lit one of the cigarettes and sat sharing it, half-choking with each drag but laughing all the while, the girl stifling the coughs with pulls from the flask but the woman refusing. When they finally rose to hike back to the hut they were dizzy, the girl a little drunk, and it took them another hour to make it home. Once they'd eaten a fast, ravenous meal, they fell together on the pallet where they slept again the whole night through.

In the dark of that second night a hound took to calling in the reed beds, a lonesome yowl not far from the women's hut. When the moon had set and the stars were draped in clouds so it turned the darkest the night could get, Buford crawled out of the reeds and up to the hut door. He eased around the side, poked two fingers from each hand into the reed wall and parted it the width of his eyeball, which he then pressed against the wall with his knuckles rubbing his cheekbones. His single eye rolling in the slit like some perverted cyclops. He saw the women sleeping, the girl sprawled like a crab on her side of the mattress and one breast exposed in the dimmest of lights. He touched himself in the dark and watched her awhile but she didn't stir and he found it hard to breathe. He crawled back to the edge of the clearing and shuffled backward into the reeds just enough to hide, and he tried howling again but it was no use.

XIV

The women woke early and piled their blood-soaked clothes into a shallow pail and set it by the door. They built a fire outside in a pit, then the girl took a pail and scooped two buckets from the pond and returned to boil the water in their big cauldron. They ate a short breakfast of what food they had left, then they stood one on each side of the boiling cauldron and tipped it steaming over the clothes in the shallow pail, the water running pink and speckled on the surface with diffusing clots of dried blood. They reset the cauldron over the fire and retrieved more water, then the woman raised up one end of the clothes pail until the water sloshed over the rim and went rushing into the yard red like a biblical deluge. The pile of clothes inside steamed in the already sultry morning.

They sorted the other filched goods into three trips, arranged their first sacks, and stacked the remaining goods into the rear of the hut. They hefted the boiling cauldron again over the clothes and left them to soak, then they hiked out to Clovis's store in the bayou. When they entered, they eased their heavy packs to the floor and leaned against the wall to wipe their brows.

The girl said, I bet you didn't think we was to find any more these days.

The woman said, And don't you go short selling us no more neither. We know now what you'd give a man and we want the same. The women sat together behind their stolen wares.

Clovis scratched his head and spat into the floor. The gimp lunged forward with a rag to wipe it.

I can't use none of this no more. I'll take what you brung but this the last load, ladies.

The girl stood in a huff but the woman pulled her seated, stared evenly up at Clovis.

What you mean, this the last load ladies?

You must not of heard. He shouted back at the gimp, Hey boy, get on back there and fetch me that stack of papers. The gimp retreated into the store. I collected a load of *Picayunes* from New Orleans. News is already old, but they it is nonetheless.

The gimp returned with an armload of foxed and wrinkled newspapers and held them up. Clovis riffled through the stack and found the date he hunted and pitched it at the woman.

The paper wailed grim headlines, the print not bold but thin and halfhearted. Surrender of General Johnston, said one. Surrender of Moseby. General Lee's Paroled Men. Booth the Assassin.

What do these mean? the girl said, reading over the woman's shoulder.

Means the war is done. Ain't no more fighting nor any need of the items y'all is used to bring me.

Who's Booth the Assassin? the girl said. The woman was reading voraciously, her finger tracing lines and her lips convulsing with the words.

Booth's the one killed Lincoln. That old ape is dead, Clovis said.

Lord God, the woman said. You see this here about Johnson and Ohio?

Yes ma'am, he's a terrible fool, worse tyrant what ever we had before. These damn fool Yankees is out for blood.

This rebellion is entirely crushed, the woman read aloud. God Amighty.

Look here, the girl said, pointing. Says Jeff Davis is heading this way, says he's heading for Texas. The war ain't over yet then, is it?

Can't you read, girl? Clovis spat. The generals done surrendered. Jeff ain't gonna fight the war hisself.

Kirby ain't surrendered yet, the woman said. And it's true they's still some men over in Texas might hold out a while yet. They might aim to set theyselves up a country of they own again, it'd be just like them.

Well then, the girl said, folding the crackling paper and laying it across her knees. Well then you might just need our services a while yet. We's close enough to Texas to be of some use to them.

Girl, I ain't interested in transnational trade, nor in going to Texas neither.

Just cause some old men got tired of fighting don't mean the young men is give up. Can't you see what this here paper is telling you? She waved the folded *Picayune* at him. They done took away all our rights, now they aim to make up new ones just to take those away as well. That Lincoln done stole you men's votes from you before he got kilt, and now Johnson say they giving votes to the black man. She pointed behind Clovis to the gimp in the corner. They giving votes to that. Folks like us is going to be ruled by niggers.

It's sad times indeed, ma'am.

It's hard times, and when men is pressed hard they fight! The woman stood up and slapped Clovis in the face with the paper like she was housetraining a dog. Them Yankees got this far by having more men than us, but they's a damn sight difference between fighting a people and governing them. That Union army would have to be a million men strong to subjugate the South. They's a lot more fighting to come, you wait and see.

Clovis laughed and shook his head, pressed his palms in the air to suggest the old woman sit. Alright now, he said, alright. They's some skirmishes left out they in the fields maybe, and maybe I got some use for these items yet, but the store's done closed after this.

They's families gonna need some sort of protection at home, the woman said. What about them that'll want they arms for keeping watch over they families?

Clovis merely shook his head. Y'all are welcome to keep the stuff you ain't brung me yet and wait for the war to rekindle, but in the meantime I wish you luck.

You son of a bitch, the girl spat.

That I is.

He collected a few sacks of food, a half-bushel of potatoes, fresh matches and some oil for their lanterns. They sneered at him when they took it.

I never understood, he said, why don't you just keep the guns and shoot for youself, whatever game you happen to hunt?

Bullets is worth more than food, the girl said, and we can't eat gunstock. A knife, a sharp stick, a length of rope, they don't have much habit of seizing up or misfiring. They're more reliable, when it come to it.

Clovis nodded at the girl, rubbed a finger over his lip and then scratched his buttock.

Course, you know they's other ways of making do out here. My usual offer is a standing one, you know.

The woman looked at him and then at the girl, stepped between the two.

What you looking at her for? Your offer was for me.

Tastes change, cherie. I find the older I get the more I like to be reminded of my youth.

The woman slapped him and shoved past the girl and out the door, stomped down the boardwalk so hard the planks rattled the whole length and somewhere a gator hissed in disgruntled surprise. The girl hurried after.

At the hut they fumed for some time, dragging the pail of soaked clothes still warm in the sun out to the pond to rinse and scrub them and rinse them again, their fists tight around the wrung skirts and uniform shirts, the knuckles bright against the dark blues and grays of the cloth and the remaining purple and fuchsia stains. They whipped the clothes into the air to shake off the water, then they carried them back to the hut to string up between two poles and dry in the warm breeze. They sat on their stump and bucket out front and watched the clothes blowing, their jaw muscles jumping, their fingers interlocked and gripped white. Finally the old woman said, To hell with it then, and she disappeared into the hut. When the door opened again, one of the packs shot out it like it was fleeing some brawl within, and another pack followed, then the woman emerged bent under the weight of the remaining packs.

Let's re-sort these here goods and figure what we ought to keep. Then we can see if it'd be worth a run into Texas ourselves.

Where would we go?

Don't seem to matter. That fight we come across the other night must of come from that direction, so I figure we head toward the Sabine, we bound to run into one army or the other.

That still feels a long ways for just a chance of coming on something, and who knows what they'd do to us either army and us just two southern women among all them men. Maybe we just take this stuff on up into Leesburg, see if anyone wants it for their home defense like you said.

That's a good idea. Maybe we do that first, then see where we stand.

They pulled apart the assorted gear, a few cook items and some personal effects like watches and tiny photographs, but most of it knives and swords and rifles and pistols. A few lever-action Spencers and one short Henry, even a Colt revolving rifle though the cylinders had fired all at once and the rifle was bloody and blown half apart. A collection of big Bowie knives many with the names of men carved into the hilts: Jesse, Sam, Pedro.

They separated all the money both Confederate and Union, sorted them by denomination and issuing country. Seventeen dollars and forty-three cents all together, though the worth of either nation's cash they couldn't determine. They stuffed the cash into a tin mess pot and tied the lid down tight. In the hut they flipped up the mattress and the woman held aloft the pallet while the girl dug a hole in the earthen floor and dumped the tin pot in. The older woman looking out the open back door at the rain barrel there.

Back out front they bundled the rifles like kindling sticks and wrapped them in a blanket and tied it, and they did the same with the sabers and long bayonets. Among the pistols they found a pair of engraved Slocum side-loaders, barely longer than the girl's hand from palm to middle finger, and they set them aside then sorted through the ammunition til they found a collection of bullets that would fit the cylinders, and they kept these revolvers one apiece for themselves. The rest of the pistols they collected in a knapsack with a few hats and some shoes. They found four mildewing books in the sundry personal effects, a Bible and three dime novels with foxed and bloodstained pages: *The Hunted Unionist*; *Zeke Sternum, the Lion-hearted Scout*; and *The Imps of the Prairie, or, The Slasher of the Cave*. They set aside the Bible then sat thumbing through the novels but soon gave up and tossed in the novels with the pistols and hats, and after considering it for a moment, the woman tossed in the Bible as well.

Alright, the woman said at last, surveying their inventory arrayed in the small yard. I think we might manage all of this in a trip, least to Leesburg. If that don't work out, it's maybe just a day's walk from here to Texas if we light out early.

I'd just as soon we get rid of what we can in Leesburg.

I accord, girl, cause between you and me, I's too old to continue this way. Tired enough now just from the sorting.

I'm wore out, too, and I need a bath. Think I'll go float in the pond a spell.

The woman eyed her, her sight flicking from girl to reeds

and back again. The girl rolled her eyes.

You're welcome to join me, if Buford's what you're thinking.

They watched one another a moment longer and then the woman sighed. No, go on, I's bushed. But you be back before dark, I'll have supper awaiting.

In bed that night, Buford and the girl both glazed in perspiration as much from the coming summer evenings as from the desperate sex they'd just disengaged from, the girl withdrew her arm from Buford's chest and faced him to tell the news.

We're gonna be gone a few days, Buford, should be no more'n two but I thought I'd tell you so's you don't come around.

Lord, Buford said, his eyes aimed at the thatched ceiling and his chest caught midbreath, I can't breathe already. You done froze me.

She slapped his chest. Stop it, now. It's just a couple of days is all. You'll live.

He didn't look at her. He hitched in a heavy breath as though something had broken loose in his throat and cleared a passage. I don't know if I will, he said.

They lay together awhile longer, then the girl sat up and began pulling on her clothes.

Wait, Buford said. Where's you going these two days of yours?

You'd follow if I told you and cause trouble I don't need. Just you stay put.

He grabbed her wrist but she twisted loose.

You can bide your time devising new ways to seduce me,

you rotten dog.

He lunged and slapped her thigh as she stood but he seemed incapable of moving farther and lay sprawled after her, gasping and laughing.

XV

In the dark, the stranger waited. The moon was up but shrouded in clouds, and he'd stripped from the Confederate uniform and slathered himself in mud to darken his skin, and with broken stalks of reed and grass still clinging to the dried cake of clay he merged without seam into the dirt bank of the chenier, another lump of earth save the dark shaft of the Sharps rifle he'd laid across the elbow of one crooked arm. All he need do now was keep still. He'd been tracking the coppery red wolf for a week and he knew as certain as he could that the wolf was in the den alone, his mate dead or trapped, gone either way. What little breeze there was he was downwind of, the Gulf sloshing quietly on the shore to the south. Sooner or later the wolf would emerge, cautious but unaware beyond his wild intuition that anything so dangerous as a man lie in wait just over the ridge.

The crack rolled out over the marsh in soft waves and sounded like no more than a branch snapping from a dead tree, though all the trees were alive and no wind blew to stir them.

The stranger carried the wolf into the marsh, to the stream where he'd set camp. He rested it by his tent, and when he'd washed away the mud, he climbed dripping from the creek, slung his small knapsack onto one shoulder and draped the wolf over the other, and walked naked upstream a few hundred yards til he found a live oak of the sort he sought. He rested the wolf to the side near the creek and he built a small fire. Midges swirled in a periphery of the smoke and a small log popped. The grass singed and shrank from the flames. He opened his sack and withdrew an oiled cloth wrapped and tied in a bundle, and he unrolled it to expose a pair of knives, one a slender stiletto and the other a short-bladed skinning knife the keen edge of which glinted in a gold semicircle in the firelight.

He lifted the stiletto and felt along the hindfoot of the wolf until he found the correct joint, then he punched a hole clear through the hock, twisting the blade once, carefully, to open it. He replaced the stiletto neatly on the cloth, then he pulled a length of rope from his pack and fed an end through the hockhole, flung the other end over a tree branch and hauled the wolf up until the pecker and testicles reached eye level. He tied a halfhitch in the rope and the wolf swung as the branch groaned overhead. He put out a hand to steady it.

With the skinning knife he sliced a pink ribbon around each hind ankle then turned the knife vertical and cut a long line down the inside of each leg to the groin. He returned the blade to the ankle of the untied leg, and he tucked sideways under the skin, and with one hand pulling gently on the pelt he set to slicing it away. When he had both thighskins hanging around the wolf's waist like torn pant legs, he moved behind the wolf and cut the pelt from the tail, the long segments of bone hanging thin and naked like the Devil's cock. He pulled the skin free of the rump and went on tugging the pelt until he'd worked it around the midsection, the marbled underside of the flesh hanging open over the swell of the ribcage, the exposed muscles pink and fibrous. He laid the knife on the oilcloth then worked his fingertips under the skin, his fingernails against the warm muscles, and he began yanking down the flesh in long rips, pivoting around the carcass as he went, stripping the wolf as one might strip a sock. The little pops of fat and tissue ripping and shushing as the pelt slipped free were a pleasure to him, and he grinned as he worked.

Soon the skin hung inside-out like a skirt so the wolf resembled a playful girl standing on her head. The stranger retrieved the knife and put his hand up under the skirt to poke the blade through the skin near the breastbone. He parted the underflesh, then he pushed one side behind a forelimb and ran a slit down the inside to the paw and began again to carefully carve away the thighskin. When he reached the elbows he untied the halfhitch and hoisted the wolf higher in the tree until its limp face hung before his own, peeking from between the cape of skin, the jaw loose and the tongue lolling between the white teeth, one milky eye staring at him. He held aside the skin and leaned to peer at the face, stared into the eye, rubbed one ear between his fingers then patted the swinging head and continued stripping the last of the skin until only the face was left. With his tongue between his teeth, he ran a slit around the shoulders and neck until he could rip the last of the pelt free. He flipped it in the air twice to shake it out, then he spread it fur-down away from the fire.

At the creek he washed his hands and shook them out but didn't dry them. He stood and pissed into the water. He flexed his fingers, shook out his arms, loosened his shoulders. Then he returned naked to the naked wolf swaying gently from the tree. He unhitched the rope and lowered the carcass til the head was in his crotch, then he took the muzzle in one hand and stretched the throat, and in one swift slice he opened the throat and the neck vomited blood over the stranger's feet. He cut again, his hands awash in blood and the knife hilt gone slippery. Deliberate, even strokes to open the neck further, further, until finally the throat splayed and the wolf's head cocked a right angle to the spine, the neckbone all that held it on. He felt with thumb and index through the mess until he found the joint he wanted, then he hacked through the cartilage and nerve-bundles and the head dropped; he pinned it with his thighs and held the muzzle tight with his one dry hand. When he got a better grip he lifted the head, dripping, with the neckhole down. He shook it once as he might shake a bottle for a final drop of whiskey, then he laid the head on the pink skinside of the pelt and returned to the creek to wash his hands again.

He sat in the dirt and watched the head for a while, the last blood congealing around the pink flesh-collar of the open neck. Then he built up the fire and pulled the head closer and sat in the glow of the blaze with the skinning knife and the head on his naked lap. He bent as he worked, turning the head this way and that to get as much light on it as he could, and he sliced carefully along the skull, holding his breath to steady his hands around the eyes, the black nose, the gums. Finally he gave a quick tug to pull the ears free, and he held the wolf's face draped over his hand, loose and misshapen before him, like a mirror. He smiled and he bent to kiss the pelt where the forehead would have been. The gory muscled skull lay still between his legs.

The women woke before sunup and ate a cold breakfast in the pink light washing in from the east. Then they gathered the packs and bundles and struck out over the reed bed into the wider marsh. They hit the shell road up along the chenier just as the sun winked over the thin horizon to blind them.

Around midday they turned north and entered Leesburg by the rope ferry over the Calcasieu, passing three black boys fishing from the bank with bent cane poles, and they followed the main road along the bend in the river, passing from building to building, peddling goods wherever they could: in the two shops they could find, at the livery, in the boarding house parlor. Sometimes on folks' own doorsteps. Some folks would take a pistol or a watch, and in the boarding house they traded all three novels and the silver case of cigarettes for a lunch of sausage and biscuits and a watery soup, but they did little business as they went, most folks too poor or disinterested or suspicious to take the wares. They gave the courthouse as wide a berth as they could, which is how they wandered down a side street and found a few more houses, one operating secretly as a small saloon.

Over drinks and haggling about rifle prices, one ancient man by the name of Isaac, grinning snaggletoothed at the old woman, waved his clawed hand over the wares and asked if they were Jayhawkers.

Nosir, the girl said. We just come upon these here in the aftermath of some battle.

The woman held up two belt buckles, one stamped CSA and

the other US. You can see we ain't particular to what we find, she said.

Isaac wheezed out a chuckle and winked at her. I can see you don't plan to reveal your loyalties neither, less'n you say you lean one ways and I turn out to lean th'other.

I's just trying to do some business, she said.

He laughed and put his bony fingers over her thin arm.

That's all right. They's talk, is all. Them Jayhawkers is causing all sorts of trouble for some folks and they's soldiers about causing trouble right back. He leaned over his small table conspiratorially, his breath foul through his gums. Just a week past, they's some horseback lieutenant come in sight of this here Jayhawker runs in the east of here, finds him and some dozen other men besides. Well this here lieutenant draws his sword and howls like a dog what treed a coon, and that party of old Jayhawkers was hotly pursued, drove all the way out to the Mermentau, where they's all captured.

By one lieutenant? the woman said.

By a crazed lieutenant and a small company of his own, yes'm. This old boy was right near a lunatic, they say. And so he got'm. They fixed theyselves a drumhead court martial, whereupon them Jayhawkers was found guilty and sentenced to die. And do you know what they did?

Isaac waited, leering between them, until the girl asked what they did.

Why they could of hung them boys, or shot'm in a firing squad, but they didn't do neither. That crazy lieutenant had'm each one tied up standing in a grove of orange trees and he walked among'm tree to tree personally slicing they throats one after another. His right-hand man nodding along like it was a test and the lieutenant was passing it. And then the lieutenant and his partner set in the grove eatin oranges just to make sure they bled out and died.

Lord God, the girl said.

Not in these parts, the old man said.

They sold a brace of pistols at the saloon and wandered back into the streets, knocking on whatever doors they found. When they passed a crude gallows hung with two black men swinging in a light breeze, one thick with bloating and the other shriveled and dried like tree bark, they knew they were entering the Quarters, a poorer section of town, where they wandered among hovels. With two sacks left and both still nearly full, they found a small tent-shop with a painted cloth sign that read Jimenez Bros swinging above the open flap. They stepped into the tent and found both proprietors behind a crude table. A couple of Mexicans, one with a mustache like a catfish and the other with one leg missing, leaning on an ancient musket, triggerless and debarreled with the butt in his armpit like a crutch. The tent looked mostly empty save a collection of farming and trapping implements and the rich scent of tanned hide and leather.

Y'all speak English? the woman said, her voice thin and dismissive.

Course, the legless brother said. What you need today?

We come to trade some goods if y'all's interested. Got us some fine firearms for defense against the coming Yankee bastards.

We ain't got much stock left to trade, can't get no shipments in from Texas til the army over there gives up, but we'll take a look. Don't need no guns though.

They bought a mess kit and a pair of knives including the Bowie marked Pedro, but that was all. In exchange they offered two steel traps, but the old woman wasn't happy and she grumbled as they left.

What the hell we gonna do with traps? They's just more work and I'd rather have the food directly.

They ain't much food to spare, the girl said, but maybe we can trade the traps on somewhere else and get us some food out of it.

But the woman groused the more as they stumbled on through the town.

As the day wore on and they neared the far edge of town, they stepped into a leaning wood structure that might once have been a cheap stilted house but now resembled more a broken toolshed. Over the door hung a sign with painted letters, Elon's Sundries. It was the last place in town, no choice left them though the woman wrinkled her nose as she entered and at first let the girl talk to the old black man in his chair by the crooked door. He sat relaxed but his back perfectly straight, vested and his top button buttoned, his legs crossed in a pair of faded brogans with the cuffs rolled up to show his workboots, a floppy bucket-shaped hat draped over one knee. His folded hands were soft with loose skin but scarred and heavily lined like old leather to show the work he'd done in his long life. He smiled at them when they entered and, curt as they were with him, he continued smiling the whole time they dealt.

We're looking for Elon, the girl said.

Elon's me, ma'am. Can I help you?

The girl offered him the two sacks and he unfolded his hands and leaned forward to root through them. We'd prefer food above most other trade, she said.

He nodded without speaking and held up the Bible to flip through, but he set it gently back in the sack. I already got me one of them, he said, and he kept rooting. He came up with a photograph of a woman and her three children posed around a chair in a parlor. The top corner, just next to the woman's head, had become dogeared, and the shopkeeper unfolded and refolded it several times like a small bird trying a wounded wing. Lordy, he said, don't they look fine. He set it back in the sack and continued.

Please, the girl said, we'd like to take back as little of this as we can, so anything you can use or sell yourself, you just let us know.

Don't go begging a nigger, girl, the woman hissed.

Elon looked at her, a brief drop in the corners of his lips, but he smiled again and sat upright in his chair. He gestured around the shop. They ain't a lot of business these days, least of all in my old store. I don't know what all I do with what you brung me but I be happy to arrange a swap, these here sacks for whatever you find of mine and we can discuss the equality of it then.

The girl took to rummaging in the shelves and boxes along the wall, but the woman stayed near the sacks. The two old folks watched each other for several long moments while the girl piled items on a counter. At length the woman cracked her lips into a cruel smile and nodded at Elon.

Just don't you get too comfortable in this here shop, boy. War ain't over yet. Just in a hiatus, is all. We'll get you back out on them fields soon enough.

I reckon not, ma'am. I's free long afore old man Lincoln

says I was. I's born free to free Creoles right here in the bayou.

You's born with the burnt skin of the Devil, darkie.

Yes'm, that may be, and they's plenty for a devil to get up to out here in the bayou, ain't they? He nodded toward the sacks. I s'pose you been up to your own sort of devilry, ain't you?

You just shut that mouth of yours and set me a price.

The girl stepped back between them and pointed to the near-by counter where she'd stacked a wickless lantern, two flasks of oil, a thick ball of hemp twine, and three pairs of boy's breeches she figured about her own size. A blackened straw sennit hat with a wide sloping brim she'd upended and in the bowl piled six bruised, lumpy satsuma oranges. A five-pound sack of dry corn.

I don't reckon that's worth what all's in one of these sacks, she said, but this is all we could rightly use. If you could sort through these here again and take what you think that all is worth—

The woman held up one hand and with the other yanked back the sack nearest Elon.

We'll do you a trade, nigger, but according to my own terms. I don't let no nigger coot dictate to me.

She opened the sack and flung out a pair of worn shoes and a kepi hat, a wooden canteen, a brass belt buckle. She grinned at the man. For the fields, cause free or not we'll get you in'm.

He looked at the small collection before him then raised his eyes.

What the hell I gonna do with a bare belt buckle out in some field?

Whatever the hell a white man tells you to, the woman said.

He laughed and crossed his legs again and waved a hand toward the door as though swatting at mosquitoes. Shoot, y'all is crazy. Y'all get on out my store afore you get me mad.

The woman screwed up her face in a fury and reached into the sack, fumbled in it with her eyes locked wide and wild on Elon while the girl watched, her own features settling into a dangerous calm. The girl reached for the second sack and began to drag it toward the counter as the woman produced a pistol and aimed it at the man in his chair.

He regarded her.

I done checked that gun already, ma'am, so I know it ain't loaded.

Maybe I loaded it, she snarled.

Maybe I can see the cylinder's empty from where I set, he said, his voice calm. His eyes flicked toward the girl then back to hold the woman steady in his gaze. His voice a level louder, he said, Missy, I'll ax you not to put none of my wares in your sack less'n you plan to put some of yours on my counter in trade.

We'll just take whatever we damn please, the woman said.

Elon uncrossed his legs and with his hands on his knees he unfolded from the chair, stood tall before the woman with her empty pistol shaking.

Y'all ain't goan rob me, he said.

The girl had shoveled what she could into the bag and she turned to the woman. Let's go now, Mother, we got what we can.

Elon reached and closed his big hand over the pistol in the woman's left fist. The hammer retracted and clapped closed, then again, the woman pulling frantically on the trigger. Don't you touch me nigger, don't you touch me!

I's just taking recompense, Elon said. He stepped forward and twisted the pistol to break it free of the woman's grasp but as he neared her she leered at him and he saw her right shoulder jerk, realized too late she'd been waiting for him to come to her. The pain in his side was fierce and hot, and with his own right hand still holding the pistol he calmly stepped backward and put his other hand over his side, the shirt slick already with his blood.

Run, Mother! the girl shouted, and with the sack swinging heavy over her shoulder she lumbered behind the woman and out into the street. The woman with her knife outheld bent to pick up her sack but Elon reached across himself and with one great swipe he backhanded her with his pistol fist and sent her reeling to the floor. He coughed once and swayed where he stood, his dark hand gleaming in his blood.

No ma'am, he said, his voice low but strong still.

The woman scrambled to her feet and with the knife raised in her fist she ran screaming at Elon but he twisted with his feet rooted on the floor and he hammered her another blow that sent her flying against the doorjamb, where she spun and sat down half inside and half out on his store's front step. He faced her but stayed put.

I done. Told you. You ain't. Goan rob me.

She looked up at him from her place on the threshold and for a moment they regarded each other. Then, blood seeping through his hand and grayfaced though he was, he advanced one deliberate step, and she rolled backward down the step hollering Save me from the nigger! but when she'd got to her feet in the road the girl grabbed her arm and they ran together out the wrong side of the town.

It took them an hour to circumvent Leesburg, another half hour hiking north along the river to find a crossing point they could wade through, the ferry too near to town for their liking, so it was humid orange dusk before they returned to the road and aimed themselves west again. They were hot and the woman's cheek was swollen and the color of a grapefruit, and she limped a little, letting the girl carry the sack by herself. As the sun set and left the sky dusted ocher, they stopped to root two soft oranges from the sack. With a folding pocketknife among their goods they got a peel going in each orange and then the woman held both while the girl hoisted up the sack to her shoulders. They carried on, peeling and slurping at the overripe oranges as they walked. They didn't talk, and they didn't hear the man come up behind them, so when he said, Howdy, they both yelped. The girl whirled so fast on him the pack slung her half around again and she lost her balance, but he steadied her.

Lord Jesus, the woman said, you scared us near out of our skin. She recognized him as the man she'd met in the plains, on the other side of the marsh, and stepped away, felt in the pocket of her dress for the folding knife still sticky with orange juice. Something about the smell of him set her off, a rank mustiness from the earth but something more than that. Almost the scent of urine, or rancid meat.

He was smiling from one to the other, his hand still on the girl's shoulder. His teeth were yellow in the last of the day's light.

Y'all are far from home now, ain't you? he said.

We just come into town to trade, the girl said as she pulled from his grasp. He nodded as though agreeing with her.

You been in Leesburg then, he said. You sent me there yourself, if you remember ma'am?

I remember, the woman said. I hope you found you a place to

stay, though I recollect you was on your way to Mississippi.

You recall correctly, ma'am.

Well this here's the wrong direction. You best head back into town, stay you another night then light out the other end if that's where you headed.

Oh, I aim to stay put a while yet, he said. See, I confess I wasn't entirely truthful with you before. I'm on my way home all right, but I have business in these parts before I get there.

Well I prefer to keep out of others' business, the old woman said.

We'll just get on, the girl said, and she and the woman turned to leave, but the straps of her sack dug at her shoulders and she reeled backward against the man, who put a hand on her shoulder and with his other held tight to the sack.

I'm afraid right now y'all are my business. I'd like to see what you carry here.

The woman gripped the pocketknife inside her pocket, put a thumb on the sticky blade ready to flip it open. She said, Well, we said we was trading, if you want to trade us.

I would indeed. How about we open this here pack. He lifted the sack from the girl's shoulders and she looked at the woman with her eyebrows high, but the woman nodded and the girl shrugged out of the straps. The stranger lowered the sack to the ground and began scooping its contents into the road.

Well, he said, well well. I see. Oh and lookee here. Finally he shook out the sack and laid it neatly aside and squatted over the assortment. Even the pistols and rifles flat on the ground slung faded shadows long down the road. The sky had gone deep sepia and in the east a stippling of stars was just winking in the deep indigo horizon. He lifted the last of the big Bowie knives and unsheathed it and turned it before his face. He looked up at the women and said, This here looks like military wares. Y'all ain't a couple of Jayhawkers, are you?

Now lookee here, the woman said. In her pocket she thumbed up the knifeblade but couldn't unfold it completely and was hesitant to move on him with the Bowie in his hand. Lookee here, we come by these on a battlefield, ain't no harm in trying to return some needed goods to our poor troops.

And which troops would those be, ma'am? He pointed the Bowie at the girl as if giving a lecture.

Which you think, the girl said, her face even but her eyes moving fast, trying to make out the situation in the twilit road.

The man stood and chuckled. His eyes seemed to gleam like flintsparks in the coming night.

The woman closed her hand over the pocketknife to hide it and pulled her fist casually out of her pocket, clasped both her hands at the front of her dirty dress in the attitude of a lady. Sir, she said, you want to trade, we can trade. What takes your interest and what can you offer for it?

There's just three or four things take my interest ma'am, he said. Mostly it's getting home, but I can't do that til I've made myself some money, so I have this second business to attend, which is fulfilling my duty as an officer and rounding up dirty Jayhawkers in these here parts to mete out justice upon them. This here looks like Jayhawking to me, and if you say it ain't I'd just judge it is anyways. So I reckon I'll just take the whole of these goods and offer you justice in return.

The girl watched the woman and waited but the woman gave

no cue. She held the pocketknife in one hand with the other clasped over it, and thus concealed, her fingers unfolded the knife, the little click of the blade the only sign it had opened. Then without warning she lunged at the stranger, but he'd seen what the girl hadn't, or had foreseen the thrust by magic, because when the blade of her knife reached him he was no longer there. The woman felt his arm hard on her bony chest, the ridge of his forearm flattening her breasts, and a cold sting at her throat, the thin edge of the Bowie firm there. She hissed and wriggled in his arm but he held her steady and she could smell his rotten breath as it came past her ear.

The girl tried to make out the weapons scattered in the road, but the light was fading and he'd moved so fast she hadn't seen, and she wasn't sure she could take up a blade of any sort in time to meet him even if she could see clearly what her options were. The moon was just slipping up over the eastern horizon, a quarter-moon but light enough once it got in the sky. So she tried a delay, crossed her arms as though unafraid and said, You ain't said your third interest.

Oh, I'm coming on it. Because y'all said y'all were looking to trade and it happens you might have something I want, for which I'm willing to trade you both your lives.

The old woman jerked hard in the stranger's arms, but he held her firm and she hissed as the Bowie nicked her throat. The girl relaxed her knees and steeled her arms, squared the stranger for the fight to come. You come to violate me, she said, you'll have to kill her first and you may as well kill me too cause I'll not let you live long after.

He grinned at her.

I believe you wouldn't, he said, but it ain't what I meant. I'm looking for men.

God Amighty, you's one of them gal-boys, the woman said, her voice tight in his stranglehold. He turned his snarling mouth into her ear as though to chew it off, but he only growled at her.

Don't play smart, old woman. I'm looking for information on a pair of men, deserters from my former regiment. I reckon you've seen them out here in the marsh.

We ain't seen them, the girl said.

How can you know lest you know who I hunt? One was a married man, and I know him to come from these parts. The stranger ran his nose along the woman's neck and she convulsed in his arms. You carry the stink of the saltmarsh on you. I could smell it on him as well, and I figure a man married is a man got cause for coming home.

War's over, the girl said. What you want with any man?

My war carries on, the stranger said. If I'm in charge of a man and that man lights out on me, I take it as a personal affront and I aim to amend that wrong. Til then there ain't no end to my war.

The woman struggled and cursed in his grasp but he pulled his forearm hard across her windpipe and what sounds emerged were only gurgles and croaks, though it was clear from her contorted face in the pale twilight that most of what she croaked were vile curses and oaths. The girl felt herself relax a bit, and she said, I think your war's overer than you reckon. This here man, he's a might short, dark curly hair, a hard broke nose like a buzzard?

You tell me where I can find him I'll be much obliged, the man said.

Near as I can reckon you can find him in a hole in the ground or in Hell itself, and you're welcome to seek him either place. That's my husband Remy you're after and he's long dead.

The man looked at her, his eyes darkly glowing in the moonlight like the ashy ends of twin cigars smoldering.

How come you to know this, he said. It was not a question.

The old woman opened her mouth in fish gestures, almost smiling herself now as she tried to answer, but the girl interrupted her. Some man he once knowed passed through, near a year ago, he let us know. That's all we ever heard.

The woman glared at the girl but ceased her labors and let it go. The man glared at the girl, too, and then at the woman who rolled her eyes to try and see him. In triune silence they regarded each other for a long moment. Then the man spat, a wad in the dirt but a thin white string remaining and slavering over the woman's collarbone.

Well that settles it, he said. He considered another moment, his gaze elsewhere with his thoughts, and then he decided. I ought to kill you both, but y'all have treated me right kindly, and I might yet find some use for you, so I'll just let you both get on. He loosened his grip on the woman and she made to tear free of him, and the girl fell to her knees and grabbed the nearest loose blade she could but the stranger was quicker, and as the old woman spun from his grasp he gently drew back an arm and sliced a shallow trench in her throat. She gasped as she staggered away from him and clapped a hand to her throat with her eyes wide and wet, the blood that seeped in pulses between her fingers dark blue and sparkling with distorted reflections of the moon on the horizon. The girl gripped her arm to steady her and held out the bayonet she'd grabbed, the woman waving the little pocketknife unsteadily before her as well. The man mimicked them, his own Bowie flashing in the night.

You, you kilt me, the woman croaked.

I've done no such thing, the stranger said. It's a shallow enough wound and long as you keep a hand on it you'll be fine. Necks just bleed, is all. He bent and scooped up a rag from the dirt, tossed it so it draped on the end of the girl's bayonet a moment before fluttering to the ground at her feet. Stop it up with that and hang on, you'll be just fine.

The girl held him with her gaze and retrieved the rag to hand up to the woman, but she stayed low herself and commenced collecting the items on the ground. The man darted forward and swept a foot at her, kicking aside all manner of weapons and she leapt away with the bayonet held on him but he'd already backed up. The oranges, still rolling, thumped wetly into the brush at the side of the road.

I'll let you go, he said, but this here is mine.

We bought them oranges, the girl said. From that Negro shopkeeper back in town.

You bought yourselves a few months more to live, he said, and you paid for them months with these oranges. Now get on.

The woman was tugging at the girl and she let go, thinking the woman wanted free for the fight, but the woman grabbed her arm and pulled her along. She had the cloth half-stained in blood at her throat, and she whispered, Come on, as though afraid speech might rend the wound in her neck wider, open her up and let it all out there in the road. Come on, she whispered again, and she backed down the road.

They walked backward for more than a mile, shuffling and

stumbling sometimes, drifting into the grass when the road bent in ways they couldn't foresee with their backs to it. They kept their blades tight in their fists, and their eyes on what of the man they could still see in the dark until at last, through bends in the road and the dim moonlight rising in the distance, they stumbled onto the thin shell road along the chenier and turned to run the remaining miles. The woman with her hand still on her throat and her elbow flapping beside her like a clipped wing as she trotted along the road and finally into the saltmarsh. By the time they staggered into their clearing and collapsed exhausted into their own small hut, it was well past midnight. The blood had dried and caked at the woman's throat and glued the rag to the wound, and she left it there through the last of the night.

XVI

When the stranger returned to his camp, he set aside the heavy sack and went to inspect his salted hides stretched across two frames he'd cobbled from branches and old planks. He untacked both hides, body and face, and he shook them out then brushed off what salt remained there. He rinsed both in the creek, then he filled an old oak barrel and a bucket with creekwater and soaked the hides.

He collected the wolf's skull, bleached in the sun, and he studied it awhile, turning it in his hands. With the skull facing him at eye-level, he traced the contours of his own face with one fingertip, then he traced the skull over the muzzle and down to the jaw. From the firepit he withdrew a charred stick and dragged a few gentle lines down the face of the skull. He licked his finger and wiped away a curve, a bend, redrew the lines, sometimes tracing his own face again and smudging himself with black ash. Then he rooted in his gear til he found a smalltoothed bonesaw, and he tucked the skull between his calves and, following the lines he'd drawn, he sawed off the muzzle.

He pulled a wire ox-muzzle from his bag and with pliers and gloves he bent it around the remainder of the skull. He slid the bone muzzle into the gaping claw of the wires and he marked several places with the charred stick. He collected a kit of augers from his tool bag and when he'd found the correct size he bored holes in the muzzle where he'd marked it. He fed the wires through the holes and pulled the muzzle tight against the frame. Then he secured the jaw as well.

He stripped out of his clothes and returned naked to the hides to haul them both out, one from the barrel and one from the bucket. He returned each, fur-down, to the frame and began to work over the flesh, breaking up the pearly tissue that remained and scraping the hides gently with a dehandled ax head. When he came to the eyeholes of the face, he dragged the thin tip of the stiletto carefully around the lids, and did the same when he scraped the lips.

When he'd finished he reached into his tent and crawled out holding a large gallon jar swirling with pale brown liquid like watered whiskey. He filled the old bucket with creekwater, then he unlidded the jar and added its contents to the bucket, the brain slopping wetly through the neck. With the headless ax handle he broke up the brains, churned them into a vile stew. He plunged the hides into the bucket and stirred them with the ax handle. Then he washed himself in the creek, stretched out in his tent, and slept.

In the morning he woke early and checked his hides. Then he built two frames over his firepit, one inside the other, and he draped the outer frame in mismatched cloths to make a smoke tent. Inside, he piled rotten limbs and balls of old moss and struck a small fire.

From the bucket he withdrew the face and gently squeezed the solution from it, then with the hatchet handle he worked again over both skins, pushed carefully outward in long strokes so the reeking solution sponged out over his knees. He added more moss and damp wood to the fire until a thick smoke poured out from under the tent flap. He untacked the damp hides and draped them over the interior frame and left them there to smoke.

He built a second fire and cooked a small breakfast of fish and biscuits, brewed a pot of bitter coffee and sat blowing over his cup as he watched the smoke tent. He drained the pot and tossed the grounds into the smokefire and rinsed his dishes and straightened up the camp. Into a round canteen he'd confiscated from a Jayhawker, he poured a measure of neatsfoot oil and a measure of ammonia, then he dipped the canteen in the creek, capped it, and sloshed the mixture inside. He pulled out the skins from the smoke tent and stretched them again on their frame, where he poured the reeking concoction over the flesh and rubbed it in with his bare hands, massaged it carefully for several minutes, grinning over the turned-out hollow wolf face as he worked it.

He covered both skins in oiled cloths and left them there as he hiked into the marsh, spiraling out from the campsite as he'd done every day since setting up. He'd decided the man he sought wasn't in his part of the marsh but until his face was ready he couldn't depart, so he stalked his own territory just for the practice.

After dinner he went into town and found the store owned by the black man. Elon was pale and laid up in his store but open for business and willing to chat, and the white man offered him a drink of whiskey to tell of the crazy witch who'd stabbed him. They talked for a while and then Elon thanked him kindly for the whiskey and the company, and the white man looked around the store and asked where Elon had got his goods.

Some come from wagons passing through, Elon said, some from folks come to trade. Some come even from that witch what stabbed me. They's over in that cupboard. But I aim to keep'm a while to remind me how foolish I is.

This here cupboard? the stranger said.

Yessir, there they is.

I'd like to buy them, the stranger said.

Well sir, I'd like to sell'm, but as I say I aim to keep'm a while yet. Seem bad luck to let'm go so soon.

I'm taking them, nigger, and I'll take no lip.

Now lookee here, Elon said, and he pulled himself upright and made to rise but the stranger turned and produced a revolver and shot him as he stood. Elon looked wide-eyed and dumbstruck at the stranger, opened his mouth as though to say something, but he continued on his forward trajectory from the chair and pitched dead to the floor. The stranger collected the gear from the cupboard and a few other things he needed, then he slipped out of town and back to his camp. He sorted through the sack, studied each item carefully and arranged them in categories of his own devising, trying to divine some sense of their whereabouts and their relation to the man he sought, but he could find nothing yet of interest.

The next day, he broke down the smoke tent but left the frame, the skins draped over it to dry. That afternoon he tacked them back to the frames to finish, and the day after he removed them for the last time and spent his morning stretching and working them smooth. After a quick supper he took a rough stone and rubbed the face to smooth it further, working the flesh side soft and loose like fabric.

When he'd finished, he hauled out the wire-and-bone mask, and he attached narrow leather straps hung with small shoebuckles to the back of the frame. He stuffed the hollow tip of the muzzle with a wad of folded leather, then he wrapped the wire inside and out with a thin layer of raw cotton and covered it in cloth and sewed it together through the frame. He donned the head like a helmet and adjusted it. He lifted off the mask and added cotton and cloth to sections inside the face, tried it again, kept working til he had the fit he wanted. Then he worked the wolf's face skin up over the muzzle, tugged it on like a sock and adjusted it gently over the face. When he had it positioned he sewed the buckles to the open back of the head and stitched up the seam under the jaw. He stripped out of his clothes and wrapped the wolfskin over his shoulders like a cape, and he put on the face and crawled to the creekside to behold his bent reflection in the water. When he saw the lupine face staring back at him, his eyes burrowed deep in the padding and black in shadow, he laughed. He laughed, and he raised his head and howled into the sky.

XVII

The woman woke in the morning with her cheek bright red and a yellow stain like spilled iodine seeping down the skin of her neck from under the blood-crusted rag. She moaned and cussed as she rolled upright on the pallet, and the girl watched her, reached to help with the rag but the woman slapped her away. The woman's neck cords strained like banjo wire and she bared her gritted teeth as she peeled at the rag, little tears in the scabbing and the rag alike, and when it came away it left fine hairs of cotton stuck in the wound and the two-inch cleft seeped a blood gooey and black like tar. She cussed and pitched the crimson wreck of a rag into the firepit in the hut and grabbed a fistful of fresh rags from a basket and stalked out to the pond. The girl followed with her bucket, stood patient to one side while the woman bent on the plank over the water, pulled at the skin of her neck and inspected herself in the water's filmy surface. She dipped one rag and wiped the wound, hissing and wincing as she did, the water running in streaks of alternating brown and pink down the front of her dress until she undid the buttons and tugged out her arms from the sleeves to drop the blouse hanging over her waist, her heavy breasts and wattled stomach striped with filthy water. When she'd got the wound clean as it would get, she clapped the dry rag over her neck and pasted it against her damp skin until it stayed, then she shoved past the girl and left her to collect fresh water for breakfast. In the hut, the girl mixed the water with the last of the dried corn to soak and boil, and she cut a few fistfuls of old cornmeal with a spoon of loose lard and added a pinch of sugar. When the corn had boiled she strained the kernels still hard out of the pot and mixed in the dough and cooked a batch of flat, dry cornbread. The woman ate only a few bites, spitting out corn kernels with each bite, before she gave up, put her hand to the rag at her throat, and lay back again to a fitful sleep.

The girl watched her a while, chewing carefully on her cornbread and swallowing the hard kernels whole, then she packed up the bowls and utensils and took them out to the pond where she washed them. She left them outside the hut to dry and peeked through the door but the woman was still asleep, so she tiptoed into the marsh until she was far enough away that she could tear splashing across the reed beds for Buford's.

He met her grinning at the door as though he'd been leaning there waiting the whole time she was gone, but the panic in her face stripped his desire as she crashed up out of the small runnel of water near his home. He retreated one foot into his doorway and when she kept coming he backed all the way in and she followed him.

You got to leave, she panted at him before the canvas door

had even dropped shut.

What in hell's the matter with you? He was holding her shoulders as though to shake her but she shook herself and he was only trying to steady her.

There's a man after you, some lieutenant, we met him on the road from Leesburg, he done met Mother already and he's asking after runaways and Jayhawkers and they say he's crazy, likes to slit throats. He slit mother's some and we might of died but he's coming here after you and you got to run.

Jesus God Amighty, slow youself girl. Here, he said, pulling her to the bed, set you a minute. He cocked his head to peer over her shoulder at the doorway then rolled his eyes to the window. He ain't followed you, is he?

No, she said, still panting. No, we met him outside Leesburg and I know he ain't followed us, but he knows we're out here.

What'd he say? Buford said. Tell me everthing.

She related the night's events though didn't mention the sacks they'd lost, one to the black man and the other to the mad lieutenant. She explained how they thought to fight but he had them beat before they even tried him, and how they'd walked a mile or more backward just to watch him but he was so fast there was no telling where he transported himself to after the night had swallowed him. She told him how the stranger had mentioned her own husband in all but name and how he could smell people and how his eyes seemed to glow in the night.

He weren't hardly human, the girl said. I thought for a time we'd been caught by Old Scratch himself.

You smell brimstone? Buford asked her.

I smelled something.

Shoot, I's just joshing you. You ain't met Old Scratch, you just met that lunatic Rougarou what Remy and I run off from.

You met a rougarou! Damnnation, Buford you ain't supposed to tell it!

No, sha, no, he said, laughing though uneasily. This here's a skunk used to be in a crew of bayou boys equally crazy. Some from these parts and some from east Texas, this one the latter. He the one we run off from in battle. I account he is indeed madder'n hell, and I wouldn't want to cross him in the road like you and that vieille done, but I ain't worried much about him. I run off from him once, I can do it again.

Why'd you call him a rougarou, though? He crazy cause he been cursed?

Not that I's aware, not no curse like you thinking, leastways. You hear stories of them Louisiana Tigers, or them old New Orleans Zu-zus fighting up in north Virginia? Well, these other boys decided to go one crazier and call theyselves the Rougarous, wore wolfskins into battle and howled as they ran, chose close-quarters to any kind of firearm, did everthing but eat them Yankees alive. Scared them boys half to hell but scared us a fair piece too, and they finally got disbanded. Old Remy and me wound up under one's command and he rode us to hell, mad as he was at having to give up his wildness. He's half the reason we lit out, might could of stood the war if not for that Lieutenant Whelan.

Still, Buford, that man is evil and I'm scared for you. And there's more of them besides? Who knows how many out there hunting you. Don't you think you ought to light out of here too while you still can?

Sha, I wouldn't survive another night without you coming to

see me. I've seen more of Hell'n I ever thought a man could while still alive, and it rode me hard in the night so's I couldn't hardly breathe. Like to suffocate every time the sun went down and spent most of my days drunk. But it was you brought me back into this marsh, the memory of you made me stay at it. You the only breath I got left, and long as you keep coming I reckon I can keep my wits and match just about anything, man or beast, what comes into this here marsh. Besides, I grew up in these parts and know a thing or two about this bayou that even God don't know.

Well I'm scared.

If you ain't scared, you ain't doing anything worthwhile. So go on and be scared, and come crawling into these here arms. He grabbed her and threw his mouth over hers as she squirmed and pushed against him, but he kept coming ravenous at her and when he finally let her go it was to push her back on the bed.

Buford, damn it, quit it. I ain't in the mood.

I made this here bedframe for you, girl. He grabbed one breast rough through her shirt. She stripped his hand away and slapped him.

I done told you to quit it. I'm in my monthlies.

He looked at her like a petulant child, surprise and fury in his face at once, then he grabbed her breast again and pinned her hand and leaned over her. She kicked and kneed at him and she cussed him as they wrestled on the bed but he would not relent, though whenever he relinquished one wrist to grab at his trousers she clawed his face and he had to pin both arms until finally, desperate, he set to rubbing at her with his pants still on. She jerked up and headbutted him in the cheek and he reeled, but she'd done as much harm to herself as him and they struggled on. She leaned up and kissed him then and he slobbered on her a moment before the shock took him and he reared back, her wrists in his hands, and leered curiously at her. She rolled her eyes and caught her breath and said, All right, at least let's do it right, and as he relaxed his grip she put her hands on his shoulders and raised up so they could roll together on the creaking cot. She sat astride him and he was fumbling at his breeches when she locked her hands on his throat and he went flailing at her arms as a moment ago he'd been flailing at his waistband. He tried to choke a protest, but she leaned into him and closed off his windpipe. He swung at her but she ducked away and he coughed once before she pressed again. They went on like this for a few moments, him swinging and her tottering back away from his fists, the two of them rocking on the cot as though indeed engaged in sex, but Buford's face was turning crimson and finally he lay back and held up his hands in surrender. She kept her fingers locked on his throat as she unstraddled him and stood beside the bed. He had a dark stain on the front of his breeches. When she released him she jumped away and he lunged sideways after her and spilled to the floor with a hard thud. He came crawling half in the bed and half on the floor until his legs toppled out after him, the sounds issuing from his bruised throat curses if he could form true words, but she simply backed away toward the door watching him come.

I said I ain't in the mood. Don't you never come at me like that again and don't expect to see me here for some time yet.

She lifted the canvas behind her and stepped backward through it, still watching him.

And don't you come around our hut nor pond again, sniffing after me, or I'll just let Mother kill you or else kill you myself. She looked at him a moment longer and added, If that Whelan finds you good luck to you both, because right now I don't know which of you is worse.

She left him there on the floor and walked home in the noonday heat, found the old woman still asleep on the pallet and fell beside her but only stared seething at the ceiling. For a long while.

Without fresh supplies, the women divided their remaining food into rations then struck out in search of sustenance in the marsh. They ran their lines for crab and fish, checked and reset the crawfish traps, hunted the chenier for bird nests in the live oaks in search of eggs. They managed a few small catches and collected a dozen crawfish, then another half dozen. The girl climbed tree after tree but the season was wrong and they found no eggs. They ventured east and north as far as they dared and in the hardwood bottoms they raided a pecan grove, their pockets and sacks bulging with hundreds of green pecans, and they spent a whole day peeling shells til their fingers were black and sticky. They kept the hulls to one side and tried to make a soup of them but it was horrid and made them diuretic for two days after.

They took to tracking wolves and coyotes in the hopes of finding them at their prey and shooing them off. They poked long sticks down snakeholes and once called a serpent up but it only poked out its head and when their shadows fell on it, it disappeared before they could grab it. One day they saw a gang of turkey buzzards circling the chenier and they ran til they were under the birds, the shadows flashing over them like ghosts and their sides cramping as they caught their breath. They rummaged in the reeds and clusters of trees til they found a shallow pit, the tendony defleshed skeletons of marsh rabbits and squirrels scattered among the larger corpse of something that might have once been a fawn. They waved away the flies and descended into the gore to pick among the bones, but they could find no meat remaining among the maggots and worms. The girl collected a handful of tiny spines into a bucket to try as soupbones but in the end discarded them back into the grave.

On the way home they heard a snuffling among the marsh and they crouched like prehistoric huntresses and peeked through the reeds to find a scrawny hound wandering in a narrow animal trail. The woman whispered, I be damned, that's old Scout, that dog those rich folk left behind. The girl looked at her and she added, Up beyond the well house.

The dog whined when it heard the woman's whisper, and the girl held out one hand, her fingers down, and she kissed at it, whistled, said, Here boy, here you come. It whined again and sniffed at her. The old woman crept a wide path around to circle the dog. It cocked an ear and listened to her go, rolled his big eyes from the reeds to the girl but she whistled louder and patted the ground. The dog nosed closer and smelled the ground near her hand but when she reached for him he shied away and whimpered. She smiled at the dog and kissed the air again, but he kept backing away. She lunged and the dog tore off down the narrow trail but the woman stepped into his path and caught him around the neck. He twisted loose and turned but the girl came up on him and he whipped around again but the old woman grabbed him by the hind leg. He scrabbled at the ground and barked and whined but she grabbed a ruff of loose skin at his neck and lifted him, nape and hindquarters, up in the air and brought him down hard in the ground. He yelped loud, a shrill echo out over the marsh, then the girl raised her empty bucket in similar manner and brought it crashing down on his head. He yelped and twisted in the woman's grasp but she held on tight and the girl set to beating his skull until it and the bucket cracked together like eggs and he lay twitching in the dirt.

The woman raised him over her head as before but this time set the body gently over her shoulders, and the two women walked smiling and panting back to the hut, where they skinned the dog and roasted it whole on a spit over an outdoor fire. They ate the hams first, right off the bone, the meat greasy and still steaming in the red light of the fire. The strings of tough meat dark and torn in hunks, and them chewing and chewing on each bite but they moaned as they ate, wiping their lips and chins with their bare hands then licking the grease from their fingers.

There was a rustling in the reeds and the girl grabbed the cane pike she'd brought with her out of the hut into the dark, but nothing more occurred until they heard a yipping in the marsh and a lonesome yowl.

Sounds like they's more'n one tahyo in the beds today, the woman said. What do you think?

I think we got enough dog already, she said, loud and out into the marsh for Buford to hear her, but if we catch that other'n we might just roast it too.

That sounds mighty fine, the woman said, grinning over her hock of dog meat.

XVIII

Lieutenant Whelan walked from house to house, from one shop to another, into the parlor of the boarding house, making his inquiries. He carried with him a handful of odd items, mostly homemade containers but a few sundries also, a clay pipe, a small pouch of old dry tobacco, a drawstring pouch made of discarded floursack that when he'd opened it had contained a fistful of mismatched bullets. At each door he asked if any recognized the items or might know where he could find their like. He wore his uniform crisply laundered and bright gray despite the few missing buttons. On his breast the coin medal newly polished. Many people saluted him, a few sneered from the shadows though they dared not openly offend him, but no one had any answers.

He followed a path that to the women would have seemed familiar, and at length he came to the tent where the Jimenez brothers sat smoking, the legless one with his stump resting on a stool and the musket-crutch leaned on his shoulder. He pressed his hands against the arms of his chair and lifted himself half out of the chair in salute as Whelan entered the tent, and his brother stood to greet him.

Howdy, General, glad to see you today, he said.

Hola, Whelan said. Ain't no general, though. Name of Lieutenant Whelan. Wondering if you boys could help me. I found these here items among the goods of a fallen fellow soldier and I'd like to find where they come from so's I can in turn find his family. I believe he come from these parts and reckon if I know where he done business I might find the rest of his kin.

He lined the items on the rough table where the standing brother leaned, and when he'd finished the Mexican poked at them, turned them over in his hands.

I don't know, he said. Business is slow these days and we ain't seen much come through our tent. He leaned and looked up through his eyebrows at Whelan, waited for a reply.

Lieutenant Whelan nodded and reached into the pouch strapped to his belt and produced a silver Mexican peso, laid it sharply on the table. Perhaps business will pick up, he said.

I'd like to see it pick up, sir, the Mexican said.

Lieutenant Whelan nodded again and reached for his belt but when his hand came to the table it held his big Bowie knife. He rested it there in his gloved fist, knocked the blade on the table a few times, and said, Maybe you ought to consider offering a discount. Might help your prospects some.

The Mexican looked at the knife for a long moment then took the coin and bit it, pocketed it, and he took up the tobacco pouch and put his nose to the opening and recoiled. He held it up before the lieutenant. I don't know if this what you're looking for, but there's a man out in the bayou sells some terrible tobacco, mostly dry and sometimes half smoked, mixed in with what he knocks out his own pipe. Sometimes he's let it go to rot and had to redry it, so you're just as likely to smoke mold as leaf. This tobacco is rancid enough to be his, though I can't imagine anyone around here would be fool enough to buy it.

Fool enough is sometimes the same as poor enough, wouldn't you say, amigo?

I suppose that's the truth.

Where can I find this man?

He sells out a old shack in the bayou a ways from here, out beyond the Calcasieu on the rim of one of them smaller lakes. Name is Clovis. I can draw you a kind of a map if you like.

For weeks the girl slept soundly and by day attended to her hunting through the marsh without disturbance, Buford at a distance as she'd ordered. But after a time her sleep grew restless and she began to hear Buford lurking in the bayou without, poking at the reed walls of the hut or making his ridiculous dog calls into the marsh. She rose one evening and went outside into the night to listen but she stayed in the yard. She hissed out into the dark, Quit it. For a while nothing happened and she turned to reenter the hut but the lone yowl came crying over the reed beds and she hissed again, All right, damn you, not tonight, but I'm a-coming.

When she returned the old woman was looking at her.

Had to do some business, she said.

I figured, the woman said. What she didn't say was, I heard.

At supper the next night, the last of the dog meat cooked in a stew with some wild onions they'd gathered in the prairie, the girl watched out the open front door as they ate, and the old woman watched the girl. They something out they what interests you?

The girl took several long seconds to answer and when she did, she refused to face the woman. I don't think there is, she said.

The two women gnawed their bones a while longer. A short drift of air wafted through the hut, two flies following it like a river current before they rose and flitted out the open hatch in the roof. The women watched the insects go, then the girl returned her gaze to the open door. The old woman asked her, You read the Bible any?

I read some when I was a girl.

Once over in Leesburg, the woman said, when I was a younger woman and me and Alphonse would go to Mass more regular, well, we was running late and ever church was already started, and as we passed that old Baptist church I overheard their preacher sermonizing about sins and salvation and how we all got to watch out. Said sinners is doomed for the pit of Hell when they die.

Only pit I know sinners go to is that old well we dump them in. What you getting at?

I heard a lot of things I know ain't true and I seen a lot of things ain't supposed to be true but was, and I tell you something girl, I believe they is a Hell. They say your body goes with you to Hell instead of resting in the ground like a pure soul's, and they it'll burn forever in these glowing flames, but it ain't to be consumed, you just sit they roasting away like this here dog forever. You might even wish you was this here dog, cooked and stewed to be devoured but it won't happen, you'll just sit they cooking still, burning and burning.

You telling me after all we done you getting religious over killing a dog?

I ain't talking about killing nothing. They's bad and then they's bad. What we do we do to survive and they ain't no sin in that. But lust? Whoo girl, you got to look out for that they lust. Worst sin they is. Sinners what lusted after the flesh in this world, they turn to animals in the next. Crawl around on all fours rutting like dogs and the brimstone burning off they knees, the skin of they palms. Some say the rougarous is lusters coughed up from Hell to walk the earth.

Now you're just making stuff up. You gonna sit there and sermonize, at least talk about the real Hell, not some story.

I ain't telling stories, I heard it straight from that Baptist preacher's mouth, and from God's to his. Lust is dangerous.

Shoot, Mother, what's got into you?

I's just telling you how it is.

A moment ago you said killing weren't no sin on account of it's necessary, now men and women laying together the way Adam and Eve their ownselves lay together, that's a sin?

That's the original sin, girl. Why it's so bad.

I thought the original sin was figuring out they was naked.

Which is what started the lust. Besides, Adam and Eve was married.

If you're talking about Buford, just come on and say so.

I's talking about what's done is done. If you done sinned with a man you can't make it right and carrying on with it is just asking for trouble. You want to get right with God and avert the punishment what's coming, you got to start over clean and let a man court you right.

I ought to start over clean from you, the girl said.

The old woman leapt upright from her seat, nearly cracked her head on the roof beam but ducked and loomed over the girl, pointing at her. She looked like an old tree, naked and half-dead in the winter leaning in the wind.

You'd of starved or else turned whore if my son hadn't taken you in, and you'd of done the same when he left for the war without me here to help you kill for a living. Now you gonna do the same for me, keep on here and help me survive til my days is done. You want to carry on with old Buford you can just go on and kill me now because I'll not see you defile my Remy's memory so soon after his death.

The girl set aside her bowl and rose to meet the woman. You seem not to mind me finding some other man to carry on with, to marry. Buford's our own neighbor and least likeliest to take me away from you, so why you prefer some other man I ain't even met yet to old Buford down the bayou I can find no reason in.

Buford let my son die! The woman was trembling, her finger jerking furious in the air. A trail of spittle slewed from her lips and fell down her chin but she paid it no mind. Her voice shook when she continued. Buford left Remy in that damn war and might well as kilt him hisself, and you'll not carry on with a man what abandoned your own husband, ma petit fils!

The girl looked at her. The woman glared back, wiped her chin with the back of her hand but seethed on, her breaths sharp through her gritted teeth. The girl shook her head.

You're a sad old woman, she said.

The woman lunged and swiped at the girl but she shrieked and ducked away, burst out the door with the woman chasing her and bolted into the reeds. The woman pursued her for several minutes but tired quickly, and when she stopped in the trail she was half-blind with tears hot and salty on her cheeks, running into her lips, snot from her nose mixing in the saline there.

The girl ran for Buford's but before she got there she changed course and headed south, her pace slowing as she neared the chenier. She climbed it to the summit and looked back over the marsh. In the pale moonlight she could see a thin column of smoke that marked Buford's shack, but she had no desire tonight to go there. She sat against the trunk of an old oak and pulled her knees to her chest and hugged them there, rested her head on her knees. She stayed like that for some hours.

When the moon had risen far overhead and the clouds dissipated enough to let the light out over the bayou, blue and swaying in the night, she climbed down the slope and struck out through the reeds. She walked the old familiar paths, passed near Buford's but kept hidden in the reeds, passed the old well with the bodies. Returned to the pond, up the path to the hut, and then inside. The old woman was snoring but she snuffled and sat up when the girl slipped through the door.

I ain't gonna leave you, Mother. But I don't mean to quit Buford lest I decide, and you can mind your own beeswax on that concern.

My son, the woman said.

That's right your son. You're right that with Remy dead I ain't got no cause to stay with you but old loyalty, and the more you press this thing with me and Buford the more you try that loyalty. You want me gone, keep at me. You want me here, you best leave me be.

The old woman was silent in the dark.

You hear me, Mother?

I hear you, the woman said.

The girl stepped onto the pallet and lay back, but neither of them slept for hours yet.

XIX

Clovis was tilted back in his chair half asleep when the door to his shack opened and let in the hot reek of the bayou. His nose twitched and he snorted and when his chair fell forward he let slip a fart. Scuse me, he said, waving his hand as he stood. He squinted in the dark at the shadow in the doorway. He waved his hand some more and looked about the shack until he found the gimp dozing at his feet and Clovis kicked him awake. The whore Marceline rolled over on her mattress and sat up swollen-eyed and drowsy with her blanket only half-draped over one shoulder, one long, veined breast lolling out over the edge like a tongue. He waved her back and she collapsed into the mattress again. Clovis looked back at the stranger in his shack, made out the square-shouldered outline of the uniform, and bowed to him.

Help you, officer?

Something hit him in the chest and he flinched. He felt his shirt for blood or injury but finding none searched the floor until he spied the little tobacco sack. He grinned and looked up at the figure in his shack.

Well, now, sir, I don't know what to do with that they sack.

You sold it, Lieutenant Whelan said calmly.

If'n I did it's done sold now, ain't mine to recollect. Now if you'd like to purchase some fresher, I can make you a deal.

You sold it to a man what deserted our army.

Clovis shook his head and returned to his chair, leaned it against the wall.

I ain't know nothing about no deserters. How else might I help you?

Lieutenant Whelan watched him a moment, then said, What about women. Two women.

Clovis poked his chin toward the whore Marceline in the back. Shoot, women I know. Make me a fair offer you can have that'n.

One was an older woman, like she could have been my own mother. The other is younger, related to the woman by marriage.

Maybe I misspoke. I ain't know nothing about no women but that'n. You want to do some business I's glad to accommodate, but I ain't in the habit of playing matchmaker.

Lieutenant Whelan stepped closer, looked around the floor til he found the stool and pulled it over and sat, leaned in near Clovis to peer up into the shopkeeper's face. He regarded him a long moment, Clovis looking down at him and growing uneasy in the silence. Finally Lieutenant Whelan sat away and reached into his pouch and produced a silver peso. He held it in the dim light to flicker before Clovis.

Let's do some business then, he said.

Clovis eyed the coin then smirked. I ain't got much use for coin out here in the bayou. I work mostly by trade.

Lieutenant Whelan considered the coin a moment then dropped it into his fist, rested his fist on his knee. All right, he said, make me an offer.

Clovis sat his chair legs on the floor and kicked the gimp. You want you a drink? Got some old bust head I could offer.

I ain't a drinker.

I ain't a drinker neither, but I do enjoy a sup. Hey boy, he said, kicking the gimp again. Get us a drink. The gimp rose and shuffled off to the rear of the shack and both men watched him go.

You seem unlikely a one to own a slave. What ails your nigger?

He ain't hardly a slave, I got him all but free. Got hisself kicked in the head as a boy, been that way since. Came to me like a stray dog, but he a good dog now.

Clovis returned his gaze to the lieutenant as though to see him anew, his presence forgotten. He surveyed the lieutenant in the dim light, then reached and fingered the gold brocaded cuffs of the lieutenant's coat. Lieutenant Whelan withdrew his arm and sat rigid on his stool.

I ain't gone to the war, Clovis said. Reckoned I's too old already, so I missed out on killing me some Yankees. You kill you some Yankees?

I've killed many a man.

Whoo boy, it must've been a treat.

Killing a man is indeed a pleasure unmatched in this world. Perhaps it's a pleasure we could share. About them women.

The gimp returned with two tin mugs poured half full of a

smokey liquor areek with creosote. Clovis reached into his cup and plucked out a twig, sucked it and pitched it on the floor. He smiled at the lieutenant. Give it some color, them old sticks, though I can't allow it helps much with the flavor. Still, it does the trick. He held out the second mug but Lieutenant Whelan pushed it aside.

I told you, I don't take a drink.

Well then, I just drink'm both.

The women.

Well, here's what I figure. I do like me that coat. He pointed to the cuffs, the corded brocade there. Them chicken guts look right smart and that medal hanging there, that genuine?

It is.

You kill a man for it?

I'd take caution with your implications, I was you.

First medal I seen in all this war. That's the only implication I make. But it'd do my heart good to tell people I served in some way. I reckon knowing where them women is at is worth that they coat and the medal with it.

I reckon it ain't. I reckon you been out in this swamp too long and done forgot what things is worth.

Well what do you offer then.

I offer you your life, friend, and recommend you take it.

They watched each other for several long moments. Clovis nodded, said, Alright. Then he looked at the gimp crouched by his side and said gently, Hey boy? The gimp looked up. Clovis said, Git him!

The gimp leapt and wrapped himself around Lieutenant Whelan's waist to pin him to the stool, but Lieutenant Whelan had spread his knees and braced his feet in a tripod and kept his stool.

Clovis jumped up and backward, his chair flying sideways and his back slamming against the thin wall so it shook, and as he reached to pull a pistol from the small of his back, Lieutenant Whelan hauled himself up from the stool with the gimp hanging on like a tantrum-stricken child. Whelan cracked the gimp on the head twice and he loosened enough that Whelan was able to throw him away into the shack. The whore Marceline rolled on her mattress and regarded the scene in confusion as though waking from some inexplicable nightmare and unsure yet whether she still dreamed. But by the time Lieutenant Whelan reached for his belt and turned to Clovis, the old shopkeep had his pistol out and aimed at the officer. He was grinning, his several yellow teeth askew. The gimp rolled and wailed on the floor. Lieutenant Whelan's hand was still at his holster.

Now, Clovis said, panting. I do wish you to remove that they coat on your own accord, cause I'd hate to have to get you blood all over it.

They watched each other but Lieutenant Whelan did not move.

If'n you take it off and lay it gentle on the counter yonder, don't get it dirty none, and the same with them fine pants, why I might just let you keep you drawers. Course I could use some drawers, but they's some mean things out they in the bayou would love to catch a man bare-assed and alone.

You think I'm alone?

Clovis peered over his shoulder at the shack door.

I don't see no one with you now.

No, Lieutenant Whelan said. Not now. Then he reached slowly and began to undo the top button of the coat. Then the next. Clovis grinned.

Lieutenant Whelan glanced at the whore Marceline still watching from the bed.

I'd prefer she not watch me undress.

You shy with women? Clovis practically sang the words. That why you after these other two, you hoping to get un-shy with them?

I just ain't used to doing what I'm about to do with an audience, is all.

Shoot, Clovis said. He turned toward the woman and opened his mouth to tell her something but before he could speak he was pinned against the wall, Lieutenant Whelan leaning hard into him. Clovis pulled on his trigger but nothing happened, and when he rolled his eyes to see, he found Lieutenant Whelan's fist closed around the cylinder, it unable to turn and chamber the next round. Lieutenant Whelan was drooling on his neck. Clovis bore down hard on the trigger and began to grunt and yowl with the effort and he felt it give, then the cylinder rolled and spat a muffled explosion and the sweet stench of burned skin. Lieutenant Whelan roared against his face, his breath hot and foul over Clovis. Then he head-butted the old shopkeep, and again, then bent and bit him in the neck. Clovis screamed and hauled on the trigger again to no avail and he felt the searing rent in his throat and then all was warm and calm, the snarling of Lieutenant Whelan barely audible above the roar like an ocean surf in Clovis's ears and the wash over his neck and chest soothing, like a hot bath. He relaxed and looked into Lieutenant Whelan's leering face, a hank of Clovis's own neck flesh dangling loose from his teeth and his chin and shirtfront painted bright scarlet, his eyes wild and alive. Lieutenant Whelan with his jaw still clamped tight began to laugh, and Clovis, unsure what else to do, began to chuckle with him in wet burbles. Then he slumped in Whelan's arms and everything went dark in the shack, and then everything went bright, and then everything was gone.

Lieutenant Whelan spat Clovis's neck flesh down onto his corpse still shooting blood onto the floor though the spurts were slackening and growing longer between, and the lieutenant breathed deeply, evenly, and settled himself. All was silent in the shack. He turned and looked about for some clue of the women, but when his eyes rested on the gimp balled fetal and terrified on the floor, the gimp erupted into wails and shrieks like a demon, his mouth stretched wide. Lieutenant Whelan watched him a moment, then he kicked him hard in the ribs, but it only set the gimp to wailing louder. He bent and took up the gimp by his throat and though the wailing kept on it was reduced now to a thin whine, choked in Whelan's grip. With the knuckles of his burnt hand he pet the back of the gimp's head like a baby, rubbed his back, said, Shh, shh, it'll be all right. Finally the gimp calmed down enough that Whelan could release his throat and he held the gimp up by his shoulders and looked at him.

Well, nigger, looks like you belong to me now.

The gimp sucked in a breath and looked about to wail again but Whelan covered his mouth and shushed him again.

You got a name, boy?

The gimp nodded, moved his lips loose and uncertain until at last he managed a word. Sssssir, he said. He started over. Yyyesr.

Lieutenant Whelan waited a moment then realized the gimp was waiting on him. Well, he said, what is it?

Tttteague, sir.

Teague? Had a dog named Teague once. Well, I tell you what, Teague boy, I'll do you a deal. You know them two women I was asking about? The old woman and the younger what bring their goods here to sell?

The gimp Teague nodded.

You ever been out of this here shack?

Teague nodded again. Yyyesr. Sometime, some sometime Mmister Clovis send me to to to watch'm.

You been to their place out in the marsh?

Yyesr.

You can show me?

Teague nodded.

Then here's my deal, Teague boy. You show me where they live and I'll let you free, just like old Abe said you was. You like to be free?

Nnnosir I, I surely die.

I think you might, boy. You want to work for me?

The gimp looked at the floor and carefully shook his head. Lieutenant Whelan laughed.

Well, what do you want?

Ccccan I jest stay here?

Seems fine to me, boy. Now get your black ass out into that marsh and take me to them women.

Teague broke into a shuffle and scurried out the door and Lieutenant Whelan followed. He paused in the door and looked back into the shack to see the whore Marceline still sitting upright and half-exposed on the mattress, her mouth agape and her eyes wide and dry in terror. She looked like she might not even be breathing. He nodded to her, tipped two fingers to his brow as though to the brim of a hat, and said, Ma'am. Then he left.

XX

Days the women worked in silence, checking their traps and lines, searching the trees for eggs, dredging up a patch of earth in the marsh near their hut and furrowing it to sow a bit of seedcorn, cultivate some onions. Nights they slept, nervous hungry slumber fraught with restive turning and uneasy dreams. But they were mostly silent, and each night the girl grew more restless, her legs wheeling in her thin sleep as though running along some ground she couldn't see. One night she writhed in vivid dream, reliving the shipwreck that cast her ashore in the marsh but with the details changed so the drowned corpses that washed ashore, bloated and white in the sun, were not of her fellow passengers but of her own parents, her father coated in the mud of the bayou where he'd actually drowned and her mother blue-skinned with a blood-flecked face from the pneumonia that had killed her. In her dream, the girl ran from the beach of bodies up the chenier to overlook the saltmarsh, but when she got there she spied a pair of yellow eyes watching her from a dark wolf den. Then from some-where distant a wild dog howled and her loins went hot as her skin went cold, and she woke in a delusional sweat unsure if she was in the hut or in the boardinghouse in Leesburg or in the well with the bodies she'd dumped there. She cried out, Mama, Mama! And as though by summons she was taken up and cradled in maternal arms, though it was the old woman's voice in her ear.

She rocked the girl in her arms on the floor of the hut and told her Shh, shhh, it be all right, your mama's here now, don't need no one but me. Her voice still raspy from the gash in her throat, but she whispered on. Her breath smelled of some smoky liquor and it confused the girl the more.

You been drinking?

Shh, the old woman said, then she sang "Hush-a-by baby" to her but when she came to the line about the bough breaking, the girl broke her grip and pushed her away, said, Stop it, Mother. I ain't your baby.

The old woman shoved off the pallet and swayed in the hut, her face gleaming in the dim light, wet with tears, then she lurched out the back door. The girl followed to the doorway and watched in the moonlight as the old woman listed out into the marsh, a heavy green bottle swinging in her fist. She only made it a few yards before she tripped on a clump of grass and fell into a shallow runnel, and the girl ran into the marsh to retrieve her. Come on, Mother. She left the bottle in the water but the woman screamed and kicked until the girl picked it up and carried it with the woman back to the hut. What the hell has got into you?

Leave the bottle, Alphonse, was all the woman said, but the girl set it outside the door and helped the old woman to bed. In the morning, the bottle was gone, where the girl could not discern, and the old woman, her head wrapped in a wet rag and moans accompanying every sudden movement, was back at her chores.

Another week passed, each night long and lonely as the girl lay awake listening to the reeds whispering in a hot breeze without. Some motion through the world to stir up souls and send them to flight. At last she could wait no longer, her legs moving of their own accord, and she crept up from the pallet and across the hut more carefully than usual, not from fear of the woman but just to avoid the fight. When she'd got outside she exploded out into the reeds, running hard and scattering sleeping marsh birds in her wake. She began to laugh as she ran.

The wind picked up, some squall brewing out in the Gulf, and it woke the old woman already distressed from dreams of her son returned from the war faceless and without wits, just a dumb smear of blood where once his features had been. She reached across the pallet to find the girl missing, and without thought she leapt from the pallet and ran toward the hut door, but upon opening it she beheld the dark red face of a wolf, huge crimson shoulders hunched behind and the hulking mass of a man-sized beast emerging through the rushes. Flash of bone-white teeth in the starlight. The creature paused and swayed on light forelimbs as though wrought solely of pent-up energy, and a low rumble near to laughter rolled up from deep in its throat. Then it charged her and she screamed and fled back into the hut. She dove to the floor and tore through their stores hunting the first weapon she could find, but the creature burst in after her and grabbed her about the waist and hauled her away from the stockpile, threw her meatily to the floor by the door. She scrambled and tried to dodge around the rouga-rou, still after a weapon, so the thing hit her hard in the face and then reached and grabbed one ankle, dragged her scrabbling out of the hut and flung her across the yard. She rolled to a crouch and made to run but the beast seemed precognizant of all her thoughts and moved with her, circling with its arms and legs wide to snatch her from her flight, cutting off her every escape. And it spoke.

Settle down, now, I ain't what you think I am.

The woman's eyes went wide and her face contorted and she began to holler. Oh Christ, it speaks with the tongue of man, Lord save us!

The rougarou lunged and tackled her and smothered her mouth with one hand and he bent to growl at her.

Stop your hollering, you'll raise the whole of Louisiana. The woman's eyes frenzied and rolled in her head like the eyes of a wild pig caught one leg in a trap and seeing the hunter's approach. The rougarou leaned in and hissed at her the more. It ain't you I'm after. I'm after that man your girl sees.

The woman moaned through his hand and muffled came her voice, I told her, I told her you'd come. Dear God save us all.

The rougarou relaxed his fingers, raised his palm away from her lips.

Where is he, this man she sees?

The woman was gasping like a landed fish, twitching under him, her head rolling as though with it alone she might wriggle from his grasp. But she answered him as she writhed. He out in the marsh.

Take me to him.

I can't, I can't let you have her.

I ain't after her neither, I just want the man.

The woman settled and looked at him, first sidelong as though looking at the sun and wary of staring directly into it, but as she calmed she noticed the canine face above her was stiff and dead-looking, the hot breath on her neck the breath of a man. The eyes buried back in the sockets human eyes, and the head just a mask. She nodded at the man and he nodded back and eased from off her, let her up. She rolled to her knees and huffed on the ground, regaining the breath her exertions and the man's weight had crushed from her, and she searched the marsh, then she raised one arm like a hunting dog and pointed frantically out away from herself.

He up the bayou, just take that they path and keep northeast and you bound to find him.

The rougarou shook his masked head. Show me, he said.

The woman shook her own head back. Nosir, I show you myself you just kill us all, me and my girl included.

What purpose would your death serve to me? I ain't interested in the likes of you or yours.

I don't trust no devil, the woman said. She stood and brushed her knees and faced him. I done showed you the way, you can find it your ownself. She looked off into the marsh to guide his gaze and then she broke into another dash to pass him but he cut her off swift as the night breeze itself, this time with a blade to her throat. She saw it as it flashed before her, recognized the Bowie of the stranger in the road. She made to touch her throat where he'd cut her but didn't want to let on she'd recognized him, so instead she put the pads of her fingers to the blade and pressed gently against it, tried to hold it away from herself. Alright, alright, she said. I'll take you in.

When the girl burst through the canvased door, Buford leapt up and began to shuck his clothes, but then he looked at her and stopped, one leg out of his pants, uncertain. She said, Go on, and began to peel away her own nightdress. He stripped quickly and they fell into each other naked, the girl already sweaty from her run.

Buford felt along her body, restrained but desperate all the same, and between hot wet kisses he panted into her ear, You missed. Me fierce. Did you?

Hush, the girl said, grabbing at him in her own kind of desperation but deliberate about it. Don't think I come running to you cause I like how you are.

Buford dipped and licked at her breast, kissed her sternum, the hollow at the base of her throat. Oh, you love me, go on and say it.

She pulled at his hair with one hand and gripped a fistful of skin on his back in the other. I don't know what I feel. I guess I need you is all.

Need ain't the word. You done betwitched me.

She pulled away and stared hard at him. Stop saying that, I ain't no witch. She kissed him then added, What we're doing is all right, ain't it?

Shoot, what we doing feels just fine to me.

I'm serious.

That old hag trying to scare you again? He pulled at her to fall on the bed but she wouldn't come with him.

She talks about Hell as if it's someplace worse than this here bayou.

Buford tugged again and this time she did fall against him but only to lay on his chest. He ran a hand through her hair, down her back, up her arm. I believe they might be such a place, but this here ain't what leads to it. People been doing this since the dawn of creation, so if this what leads to Hell it must be overfull by now and ain't no room left for the likes of us.

Buford, I'm serious damn it.

So's I. Sha, if I had to go to Hell just to be with you, I'd do it.

She ran a fingertip over one of his concave hairy nipples, traced the hard shape of his collarbone. You just want to lay with me is all.

He raised her face to his so she could see him. No. Now I's serious. I do want to lay with you but I also want to be with you. I's tired of all this sneaking. Let's you and me get married.

You serious?

I declare myself for you, yes ma'am.

With a pistol cocked and aimed at her back the woman led the rougarou through the marsh, and they were silent as they walked. The wind kicked several times and in its ebbing still blew enough to stir the reeds into a soft applause. Sometimes they heard other sounds as well, the splash of a gator into the water, the yowling of an owl out in the distance. Finally the rougarou spoke.

This here marshland seems sometimes endless, don't it? Ain't no telling what all manner of evil lives out here. Snakes, gators, demons, witches.

Monsters like youself.

The man laughed, the sound hollow in the bone of his mask.

Yes ma'am, I'm a monster. No different than any other monster walks the earth in a man's skin. Or woman's too.

They continued several paces and then he added, You judge quick for what you know. You seen what this war was. Look around you at what we done to ourselves.

You seem awful proud of what you is, proud your evil is of a human variety. She stopped and turned to face him in the night. Why you dress it up the way you do?

He cocked his head like a dog and for a moment the maw of the dead wolf looked like a smile. He said, Makes me look awful fierce, don't it?

Not fierce enough, I reckon. Your boys didn't help us finish off them Yankees, and now you out here robbing simple folks and harassing old women. Can't even hunt you a man without a woman's help. What purpose you got to look fierce anymore anyhow?

You're right ma'am. I've seen many of my boys die out there in battle, I've seen plenty more run off from me unafraid. Like your own boy. She started, made as though to move on him but he raised the pistol and she froze. I know that deserter was your son, the one you say's dead. Left me to fight this war myself and lit out to hide in this here marsh.

You son of a bitch.

Like this other fella we hunt now. What kind of ferocity is there in a commander who loses men thataway?

The woman shook her head and glared at the man in the dark.

What you men deserve for starting this war in the first place. Them Yankees should of let us alone for true, but we should of just walked off in the secession and let the North sort theyselves.

We took Sumpter fair and easy and that was that, but that weren't enough. Way I hear we the one's moved up on Washington and got them Yankees all stirred up, and now look at us.

She put her hands akimbo and beheld the man. Looked away as though distracted by something. Looked back at him.

All you men. Too scared to leave things peaceful and live your lives, you gotta go make a war and kill youselves just to prove you ain't afraid to die. Afraid to live is what it is. Afraid to let others live they own lives, too. Now here you is afraid to let old Buford live his own life, you gotta hunt him just to prove how mean you is.

For a moment they only faced each other, and when the rougarou spoke, his voice came cold and monotone:

Woman. You want to know why I really wear this here face?

She watched him til he continued.

I've seen what we truly are in this war. You haven't. You think you know what's happening from what stragglers and deserters come through here, what news you read what's written by folks ain't even in this war. Some fancy writer out on a hill scribbling away, some special drawing a pretty picture. They haven't stabbed a man through the heart. They haven't shot a man knowing they're about to be shot themselves. I've seen death in front and behind me, I've seen death inside me. I and I alone know what living is, and what it's worth. I wear this here mask not to hide what I am but to show it. This ain't no disguise of ferocity, it's man's ferocity unveiled.

They watched each other a long moment more, and then he waved the pistol at her.

Now get on, show me where we're going.

She did not move. He aimed the pistol at her and she crossed her arms and then she spoke.

In reward for showing you to old Buford, I want you to take off that damned mask. I want to see you face Buford as a man and I want to see you kill him that way.

I am what I am, and I aim to face Buford in my own way. Now you get on.

In all my long years upon this earth I ain't never seen such cowardice.

They faced each other. Then the man stepped forward, slowly, and as he came he raised the pistol.

The woman didn't move.

When he reached her he pressed the muzzle lengthwise and warm along her cheek like a finger to caress her. He did caress her.

She stared into his eyes and he into hers.

He said, Ma'am, when we get to Buford's, I will let you and your daughter leave so I might kill Buford leisurely and in my own fashion, and that'll be the last we see of each other. But if you don't move this instant I will find that girl of yours and I will return for you, and you know that I'll find you sure as I found you tonight. And when I do I'll shoot you first. In your knees so's you can't run off. And then I'll let you watch while I do things to that girl even the Devil himself ain't imagined. Not because I think you'd care but just to show you what I plan to do to you once I kill the girl. Except when I'm done with you, I'll let you live.

They regarded each other a moment longer but he could see in her eyes that he had only to wait now, and when a moment more had passed, she turned and walked unsteadily on through the marsh. They continued the rest of the way in silence unbroken even by the call of birds.

When at last they slowed, they came out into a clearing and the man stopped and raised his nose, the nose of the wolf, as though actually to smell the air. The woman had brought them into the old homestead, the maw of the well reeking in the dark.

God Almighty what is that? the man said.

That the scent of death. I thought a demon such as you would of knowed it better.

The rougarou raised his pistol at her again. This ain't where Buford lives.

The woman put a finger to her lips. Keep your voice down. She stepped closer and he cocked the hammer of the pistol but she came on, cautious but deliberate, and she spoke in a hoarse, lowered tone. This is where my girl and me done dumped our own bodies. She gestured toward the well. Me and her, we know death same as you, we stabbed plenty a man our ownselves. So you come for us you better kill us outright and not mess about with no fool games like you talk, cause ain't neither one of us would leave you alive. Knees blowed off or violated or whatnot, we'd kill you same as these men and dump you here to rot.

He lunged at her and pressed the barrel to her forehead, one hand behind her neck to steady her skull against the pistol. I'll kill you now, he snarled.

Go on, though you'll want to be quiet about it, seeing as how this here is where Buford sleeps and you'd just scare him off.

He don't live here.

Sure he do. Says the smell keeps folks like you from poking about.

There ain't no house here.

Ain't got no house. That fool done burrowed in like the snake he is, dug hisself a home in a kind of cellar under what used to be the house. Says thataways you don't even know he's here. You let up, I'll show you to the trapdoor what leads to him.

The rougarou relaxed the pistol, considered her a moment, then stepped away. The woman crept to the old foundation, felt around in the dirt until she'd found half a discarded brick and she reeled up and ran at him and before he could raise the pistol again she'd crushed the brick into the side of his mask, sent him reeling backward. The gun fired as he fell into the dirt and she raised the brick again, but he got his bearings and aimed the pistol from the ground. She threw the brick and it knocked the mask askew to blind him, then she sprinted to disappear into the marsh. Ran and ran, first sidelong then out and up onto the chenier and through the woods there, then down and back into the marsh, winding a meandering pattern through the saltmarsh to throw off the rougarou. Then she headed for Buford's place.

She burst into his lantern-lit shack but found them both gone. She ran out onto the porch and scanned the surroundings, then she rounded through the yard, peering into the reeds about, but she found no trace of them. The wind blew. She thought to run for her own hut but worried the girl would return to Buford's first, and she didn't know what to do. Then she heard laughter, high light giggling and a heavier laughter and she whirled to see Buford and the girl after him part the reeds and dash into the yard both naked and breathless. When the girl saw the woman she threw one hand over her groin and an arm across her breasts, but Buford just laughed the more and put his hands on his hipbones, his dark prick loose and heavy from its wiry tangle of hair.

Mother, the girl began, half fearful and half furious in her tone, but the woman waved her away and gestured them both inside.

We got to get off the bayou, she said, I done seen something you need to know.

I bet you seen something, Buford said, but the woman ignored him and slipped back into his shack. They followed a moment after, and the girl dragged the thin blanket off Buford's bed to wrap herself while Buford sat in his chair and lazily pulled on his trousers.

What is it, Mother? the girl said.

She ain't your mother, said Buford from the chair, but the woman wouldn't look at him.

I done seen the rougarou.

The girl gasped but Buford laughed and laughed, slapped his knee.

Whoo, shit, you still trying that old story?

Damn it, Buford, he coming for you, the woman said. He says he used to command you and Remy and he the one you run off from.

The girl more terrified now than before turned to Buford with huge eyes and whimpered.

Buford shook his head and said, Well go to bed, I'd never of thought it. He really come all the way in here?

He did and he aims to kill you, so if you know what's good you'll get to running now, this very night.

You seen him, the girl said.

I did, I only just escaped.

How come you still alive? Buford said. He was leaning back

in his chair, his arms folded on his naked chest.

He held me at gunpoint and told me to lead him to you, and for true I'd of done it cept I knowed she was with you. I led him out into the marsh and ran for it, lost him and came here to warn you. She looked at the girl. This is the end for us, girl, we got to get back to the hut and grab what we can and get before sunup. They ain't no more life here for us.

The girl grabbed for her dress and turned her back to haul it frantically on, but Buford just chuckled.

Y'all is motier foux the both of you. He just some old skunk I lit out from once, now he ashamed to of lost me. I ain't worried none about him and neither should you.

Buford please, the girl said. Please, you gotta run, you gotta leave tonight. He'll kill you for sure.

Buford stroked her face as the woman grimaced at them. He smiled and said, He just a man like any other, you and me can kill him together.

The woman sneered, but then an idea occurred to her and she leaned over them both, her bony face carved in shadows from Buford's lantern light.

He might of seemed a man to you at times but he done struck a deal with the Devil, and you can try and kill him if you want but they ain't no killing this one.

What you talking about, vieille?

I seen him, only barely escaped. You can't kill this'n. Drawn blood ain't enough—he owned by Satan and'll keep coming back from the dead to hunt you. You and her alike. All of us til we's dead.

I done seen what's possible in this world, woman, and I'll

tell you, if I can kill fifty men once I can kill one man fifty times. He come for me over and over, I'll just keep on at him til he give up and goes on to the afterlife.

It don't work thataways, the woman said.

It don't work any ways you could think of. Nothing does anymore.

He turned to the girl and held her by her shoulders.

That old woman's right about one thing, sha. Til I get shut of this old skunk, you best stay shy of me. He glared over the girl's shoulder to the woman, said, Don't you go nowheres, though. I'll be finished with this fool rougarou fore you can even get packed, and then I's coming back for this'n.

You survive a week, you can have her, the woman said.

XXI

The sky hung heavy with clouds piling up gray overhead, a
sheet of them out in the Gulf sweeping away over the horizon though the air over the marsh lulled still and sticky. Buford
and Lieutenant Whelan circled each other for three days in the
marsh, each always on the other's trail. At night they bivouacked
without fire and each ate cold meals of hard tack mostly on the
go, as though back in the field at war. After the second day Buford
considered returning to his home and letting Whelan come to him,
but he decided he had no defense better than to keep Whelan in
motion. On the third day he left the marsh and rose up onto the
chenier and, hidden in the upper branches of an oak, once caught a
glimpse of Whelan loping through the reeds. Then he slipped from
sight and Buford climbed down and circled back into the marsh,
thinking to cut Whelan off and surprise him. When he came to the
small clearing where he'd seen the tiny wolf's head flash in the
marsh, he scanned about then looked up to the chenier to check

his position relative to where he'd been, and he caught another glimpse, this time of Whelan dropping down the slope from Buford's own former position and returning into the reeds.

On the third afternoon Buford returned to his house only long enough to collect new food, and in the night he continued his maneuvers. He waited until after dark then backtracked parallel to his own path hidden in the reeds. He crept along in gradual progression, barely a step between breaths and every footfall measured in the reeds so as to disturb nothing. Every few yards he paused and listened. The moon was thin and the heavy clouds masked and unmasked it in strips, and he would wait in each lighting to scan his surroundings. In this way, shortly before dawn with the sky pink with a sickly light, he heard the morning preparations of Whelan in the reeds some dozen yards away.

He knelt in the reeds and shifted silently until he found the thickest cluster in the lowest depression nearby, and he crawled to it and squatted to wait. For a while nothing happened. No sound hinted at the events to come. Then a white egret bolted into the sky and shuddered off overhead. Buford craned his neck to see its origin and so determine the position of his foe, but as he did so he rustled the reeds that closed on him in a mantle, and in that moment both men rose and found each other. They both charged screaming at the other. Whelan still adjusting his mask as they ran.

They met each other in a violent embrace the force of which sounded like a muffled thunderclap. But Whelan had not yet secured the buckles on the mask straps, and when they collided it came askew on his head. Buford slapped the muzzle to spin it further and so blinded Whelan. He took to pounding Whelan's midsection until the rougarou gave up on the mask and blocked the blows and shouldered at Buford blindly. When Buford backed away to reach for his knife, Whelan took the reprieve to rip off the mask. He growled as he leapt onto Buford.

They wrestled in the marsh. Rolled through dried clay and into rank pools, punched at each other. Whelan clawed at Buford's face, ripped open long gashes and Buford let him do it, because he needed one hand to keep up the fight and the other to at last reach his knife from its belt. Whelan did the same and they stabbed each other at the same time. Buford shocked in a gasp by the sudden rending of his flesh—Whelan howling and grunting. They went to stab each other again, but Buford rolled Whelan off to clutch at his side. Whelan pounced again and fell this time on Buford's knife. He seemed unconcerned and slashed at Buford, hacked at him with his thin stiletto in short sharp jabs. He stabbed the clay as often as Buford and hit Buford mostly in the arms and shoulders, but Buford just held on. He dragged his buried blade through Whelan's chest. Felt a snag and a pop. Whelan's eyes flew wide and he gasped, spat blood over Buford's face, and they both realized then that the wheezing issued not from Whelan's lips but the ragged hole between his ribs where his lung had collapsed. Whelan tried to scream but couldn't. He cast himself sideways off Buford and clutched at his ribs, and Buford rolled away to press against the bleeding of his own wounds.

They groaned on the ground, but Buford was the first to roll back toward his foe and Whelan reacted too late. Had only time to raise his knife as though in offering as Buford staggered to his feet and stepped on Whelan's throat. Whelan flailed on the ground and swiped at Buford's calf. At first he only slashed shallow cuts in Buford's pant leg. Then he switched his grip as though holding a fork and stabbed into Buford's shin. The blade scraped against the bone then slipped between tibia and fibula and protruded a half inch through the calf muscle. And Buford cried out, no animal yowl but a wail and then a shuddering bawl, tears falling pink with blood from his face over Whelan's purple head. But instead of falling off Whelan, Buford leaned forward, catching his forearms on his bent knee. Whelan's windpipe crunched, a sickening sound followed by a multitude of sharp cracks from his vertebrae. He spasmed in the dirt and then lay twitching, his eyes clouded with blood from his burst capillaries, his tongue bitten half off between his teeth. Then Buford fell.

It took him half the day to limp and drag Whelan's body to the well by the abandoned homestead, and when he finally managed the strength to tip Whelan over the lip and into the well, he cried out and fainted from the pain of it. He woke sweating thirty minutes later and simply lay there, waiting. Soon he fell asleep again and didn't wake til evening.

As the sun touched the tallest distant trees, he ripped the last of his shirt into strips and bound his blood-crusted calf, then he crawled out of the clearing and through the marsh like an alligator, made his way back to Whelan's bivouac site where he found the bloody knives and Whelan's mask and a small pack. He threw the mask and knives in the pack and dragged it half-crawling back to the well. He pitched in the mask and sat with his back to the stone wall of the well sorting through the pack in the dying light. He collected the few things he thought he could use and then tossed the remainder item by item over his shoulder into the well.

He slept there on the open ground though he woke several times with his shin hot and screaming and screaming himself from some nightmare unremembered.

The girl found him the next day still slumped by the well. He vomited when she woke him, as much from the smell as from the pain in his calf. She helped him to his knees and then hauled him onto her shoulder and dragged him back to his house where he collapsed. She bathed him and dressed the wounds and stayed the night. When he woke in the dark he touched her face, and though his voice came raspy and painful in his throat, he said, I's sorry about these scratches.

Hush, she said.

I thought I could stay handsome for you, but I guess you stuck with a ugly old dog.

I'm stuck indeed, she said. You think this is bad, you'll find yourself in a world more hurt you ever try to unstick yourself from me.

He laughed but it hurt so he quit.

Least we can rest easy together, he said.

You killed him?

He dead.

Dead for sure? You checked?

I dumped him in that old well of yours. He wants to come back for me he gonna have to crawl his way out of Hell first.

You look like you're crawling your way in. She dabbed his head with a cloth and said, Sleep some more now.

In the morning she left him sleeping and ran to the hut where the woman sat pounding cornmeal in a bowl, the muscles in her old arms tight with fury.

He done it, Mother, he done killed the rougarou.

The woman snarled up at her.

They ain't no killing it girl.

He said he dumped him in the well where we dump ours, ain't no coming back from that alive or dead. It's done and over.

Well don't look so happy. Ain't no telling what God or the Devil have in store for you two.

You listen here, Mother, I done had enough of this. It'd for true take one or the other, God or the Devil himself, to keep me and Buford apart now, and you just better mind your own beeswax from now on.

I ain't getting in the middle no more, the woman said, pounding the harder at the cornmeal nonetheless. I ain't fool enough to come between you and the Devil. You on your own now.

The next day the old woman let the girl run off to tend to Buford, and she packed a small sack with rope and took up one thick branch from their spit and a heavy log and hiked out into the marsh. She headed for the well.

The stench from the well choked her, and as she let down her sack, she pulled her dress top up over her face, then she reached into the sack and took a cloth and wrapped her nose and mouth like a bandit. She raised up the spit branch and jabbed it into the earth near the low wall, worked it back and forth to drill it several more inches into the ground. Then she used the heavy log like a club and set to pounding on the spit, driving it into the earth. When she'd got it leaning stiff against the well, she extracted the rope and began looping it over the spit below the fork in the branch, tying it in some elaborate and unnamed knot. Then she pitched the remainder to uncoil down into the well.

She hiked her skirt between her legs and tied it off then straddled the rope and climbed into the mouth of the well to descend into the gory deep. The walls were rife with some slick mucus and the flies that swarmed about her seemed furious at her incursion. She gagged against the reek. When she reached the bottom and dipped her feet into the rank surface of the water, she shuddered and choked back the bile that welled in her throat, but when her feet slid against the grimy surface of some body, the skin down there wet and furry like lake slime, she couldn't help herself and she lifted her mask and bent to vomit into the water. Still she pressed on, lowered her other foot and slid around in the murk, dry-heaving and trying to ignore the soupy vomit that sluiced around her calves. She steadied herself and got a foothold on the piled bodies in the water and squinted her eyes in the dim light until she could make out the freshest corpse among them. He was barefaced and staring up at her, his grimace pallid and his stretched throat swollen and black so he looked like a disembodied head in the dim light, and she heaved again but didn't vomit. He was naked save his befouled drawers and a yellowed undershirt and some sickly flap of hide floating under him. She tilted him up from the water and tugged and was finally able to pull free the soaked wolf pelt by flipping the dead lieutenant over, his head flopping loose as a dead chicken's. She choked back bile and searched anew, bent and swept her arms, cringing as she reached into the water, but at last she found the sack with his uniform still in it and the mask dripping and half-broken in the mire. She pulled them out and put the mask and pelt into the sack and tied it to the end of the rope, then she looked back at the overturned lieutenant. She put a hand to her mouth and looked at him for several seconds, then holding onto the rope she kicked him with one foot.

You son of a bitch, she said. I hope you happy down here in this hole. She lifted the flap of her cloth and she spat on him. This here's as close to peace as you ever get, but at least down here you among friends. Foes too, I suppose, but you all the damn fools what got us into that war and you deserve each other. Her eyes burned and her chin quavered and she thought she might choke but she swallowed dry and hard. You the one kilt my son, she said in a shaking voice. You and that fool Buford, and I reckon you got off easy getting pitched down here.

A low moan sounded in the hole and the woman gasped and clapped her hand over her mouth. The light was thinner, watery, and she peered into the murk but nothing moved. The moan came again and she looked up at the circle of sky overhead as though to pray but saw that the light had gone green and unearthly. The wind was rushing overhead and she could hear now the violent dancing of the reeds in the marsh. Far away there came a gentle roll of thunder. Lord God, she said, and she spat on the lieutenant again then turned to the rope and began her ascent.

She took twice as long up as the climb down, weak and shaken, but when she'd got out she turned immediately and hauled up the sack after her. Already the wind had driven up enough that she had to steady herself against it, and she turned to look out in the direction of the chenier and the Gulf beyond. The hard ribbon of clouds rotating out in the distance was the color of quenched iron on an anvil, dark steely purple and roiling with heat unseen.

Oh Lordy, here they come, she said, and she shouldered the sack and jogged into the reed beds toward home.

The winds blew fierce and kept increasing, yet even above

their roar and the swaying rush of the reeds she could hear a darker rhythm, the pounding of a heavy surf against the shore off over the chenier. Halfway home she changed course, veered north and ran for the fringe of the marsh, headed toward the bottoms.

By the time she got there the rains were coming hard and she slung the rope she carried high over a pecan branch and hauled up the sack. She leapt into the tree and climbed out on the branch, the wind creaking in the tree and swaying her as she inched along her belly to the loop of the rope and when she got it she dragged up the end and flung it several times around the branch to tie it down.

The tree rocked her and the winds were beginning to howl. From high in the tree she gazed out toward the marsh and beheld the reeds swept flat like combed hair and zipping so viciously from their roots she thought at first she was looking into water, the Gulf already come to flood and rushing in a violent current toward her. She wrapped herself arms and legs around the branch where she clung like a squirrel and she inched her way backward, the limb creaking dangerously and the bark already slick in the driving rain.

The sky was iron and gone in a dense haze of downpour not a hundred yards away, and when she shimmied onto the trunk she slid fast as she could down it and dropped the last eight feet in a freefall, herself born a foot away in the wind. She crawled against the wind as though fighting a river current and she forced her way back into the open marsh, where the gale blew unimpeded and she had to keep almost on all fours just to stay rooted to the ground. By the time she got into her part of the marsh the pools and ponds had risen and she was wading in water to her calves, sometimes to her knees. She kept her eyes on the rushing water looking out for snakes.

She made it back to her hut but found no sign of the girl and the water was already a foot deep inside. She rummaged in the murk and grabbed what she could—an orange, the old bayoneted musket, a knife, a blanket tied into a bundle with the rope for straps—and she ran out into the marsh again. She headed for the higher ground of the chenier, but as she neared it she realized her mistake. The oaks along the ridge were writhing like tortured epileptics in the winds, and she could make out through the thick rain a cascade of water like a cataract come roiling down the inside slope toward her; a vast arching spray exploded bright against the dark sky as the Gulf slammed over the chenier.

She turned and ran east with the wind at her back, crab-walking north when she could manage it. She emerged onto the prairie, the lowland woods overshot by a half a mile, and as she veered north and battled against the gale she slipped in the mud again and again. When she at last managed to claw her way into the woods and the thin shelter of the trees, she looked like a mutant rat, undead and disinterred and sent ravaged into a living Hell. She waved her arms ahead of her nearly blind as she walked; the big pecans not twenty feet ahead would be there and then they wouldn't, disappeared behind the violent veil of rain. She knew the woods would offer no haven, fragile in the wind as they were, but at least they broke the driving bluster enough to let her hike upright as she made her way east toward Leesburg in search of the safety of some rooftop, if any roofs still remained. She never made it.

The tempest roared about her interminable and furious, the torrents of rain driven against her by a fierce and indecisive gale that whipped at her from every direction. The water rose and rose and then in a rumble as though of some monolithic thunder she felt the ground tremble and she scurried up a sturdy tree, climbed high as she dared. Then she saw the wall of water charging toward her in angry white waves from the overflowed Lake Calcasieu, and she clawed at the bark and pulled herself higher still. The tree bent with the force of the flood and she clung to it like a lover, herself hanging almost diagonal over the torrent.

Several minutes passed and she began to elevate as the tree adjusted to the wash but then it shuddered and jumped and she stared walleyed down into the water as great masses of ripped timber and the wreckage of homes and cotton mills and sugarhouses dredged up by the angry flood slammed against and slewed off the trunk. Several times the jarring slid her down by inches closer to the raging water and she shinnied her way back up, and she clung there shivering, her face twisted in agony through the night.

In the reed beds, the storm ripped open as Buford and the girl slept. Buford limped to the window and craned his neck to look upward, but he saw only a high veil of pale clouds looming calm and unconcerned and could not account for the whine the wind was making in his roof. When he went to the flailing canvas door to peak out his head, the wind billowed the curtain like a sail then ripped it from its frame and sent it flapping away like a wounded raptor. He dove after it with one hand on the frame and when he looked into the sky he saw a high purple wall darkening black and curving out over the horizon and bearing down on the marsh with unnatural speed. He yelped when he saw it. He wrenched himself back indoors and hollered at the girl to get dressed.

He grabbed his broadax and a long pole and he set them in the far back corner. Then he grabbed his small table and gestured to the chair. Come on, he shouted to the girl, and he hobbled to the door to pitch the table into the yard where it tumbled like dry weeds off into the marsh.

The girl stood holding the chair and shouted at him, What the hell you doing? but in answer he simply grabbed the chair from her and pitched it out too.

Then he leaned into her ear and shouted, That wind gonna rip through here fierce and all this stuff'll do us nothing but injury. He began collecting other small items and pushing them into sacks, but when the girl went to toss one sack out the door he grabbed her arm and took the sack from her. He threw it on the bed with various other articles, then he hauled up the short end and began to roll the tick mattress over the goods. Come on, damn it, he shouted, help me! Together they rolled the tick and she held it while he took up a rope and tied it in a thick bundle. Then she helped him lift the unwieldy bedframe and, shuffling slowly against Buford's re-bleeding leg, they carried it tilting into the yard and dropped it.

The storm raged in torrents, the flashing sheets of rain piercing like glass shards even through their clothes. The shack groaned and as they fled back to it they were arrested by a sharp crack and then the whole face of the house, doorframe and all, sheared off and trundled into the reeds. They ducked and cried out the both of them, but Buford grabbed the girl's hand and dragged her into what was left of the shack. The roof fell in after them like the maw of some beast devouring them whole, and then the reed thatch, loosed from the broken structure, went zipping away in receding lines, the roof unraveling like a rug until barely half of it remained.

Buford went from one corner to the other among the three remaining walls, determining from the deluge the sturdiest section left on the shack, and there he wedged the mattress-bundle. He handed the stiff pole to the girl and he took his broadax and they collapsed seated with their backs against the tick and waited in the raging storm.

They had sat breathing heavily only a few minutes before they saw the rush of surging Gulf water crash past the open end of the shack like an undammed river. A great sluice of it climbed the porch and ran at them, and the girl pulled in her feet but suddenly the whole shack reeled, the back side where they sat dipped violently and the open end tilted up so all they could see was dark gray sky and the rain rushing in the front hole. The girl caught her breath and held it, but both she and Buford kept silent. Something knocked against the underflooring and then a heavy wooden crash slammed against the side wall and set the shack spinning on its corner until the water lifted them free.

A rattle like bullet fire pounded on the house and Buford gasped and put his hands over his ears, the wide head of the broadax fanning beside him and the handle waving out before his face, and he began to hyperventilate. But it was only a thick hail. Lightning flashed again and again but above the shriek of the wind and the pounding hail they never heard the thunder.

The shack groaned as it rocked in the water, then part of the wall opposite them ripped loose and folded back like paper, then tore away completely, leaving the sodden bousillage daubed between the timber studs until the mud melted in the rain and the crudded balls of moss fell away in chunks, just the posts standing open on the wall like unsailed masts.

The house dipped and sloshed maniacally and they were racing in a new-formed river born of the Gulf, and for a while they only held each other and watched. Then in the dark distance ahead they first heard and then beheld a crash of surf and spray in the water. Oh Lord, Buford shouted. That's Lake Calcasieu done jumped its banks—these two currents is merging. Hold on! But with nothing to hold on to, they simply continued clinging to each other.

They hit the wall of rapids in a spray of foul, salty water, the shack floor tilting dangerously and the mattress shifting against them as they slid toward the edge, but the whole structure rocked and pitched as it spun and they skidded and tumbled over the center of the floor, managed to hang onto the mattress bundle and keep it with them. They spun in long crazy ellipticals in the water for several long minutes until finally they'd settled into a diagonal course up the submerged marshland, and with the girl doing most of the lifting they managed to shove the mattress back into the safety of the one good corner and they huddled there with it, blood from Buford's calf pink on the wood floor.

They rocked and rode the current and watched through their two open walls as items floated past them from Leesburg, many with their own passengers in refuge from the storm. A wooden crate of oranges and a gang of fruit loose and following like ducklings, a thin snake coiled in the crate and seemingly asleep. A wardrobe on its back and the doors flung open, with a dog inside peering overboard wide-eyed and panting with his tongue out. An uprooted sapling with a cow tied to it, the cow choking on the leash and thrashing in the water.

A little while later they saw an old black woman, tiny and frail with her hair the color of brushed steel and her skin heavily wrinkled, floating on top of a haystack somehow still intact. She waved to them and called out for help, but neither Buford nor the girl moved. They regarded each other, the pair and the old woman. Then the old woman shook her head and shouted across the water, Well, thass all right, God bless you anyways. And she floated on.

Later they caught up to and passed the tied cow. The cow was dead.

A locked trunk floated past and Buford watched it a moment as it drifted near them, then he scuttled across the floor and slung out the ax and chopped at the trunk. His first swipe missed and the ax went into the flood like an anchor and nearly dragged him after. The girl screamed, but he held onto one of the wall-less stud timbers and brought the ax around and hooked the trunk and dragged it aboard. He hacked at the lock then ripped up the lid to find a collection of fine dresses wrapped in muslin. The interior layers were still mostly dry, and he hauled out all the clothes then kicked the trunk overboard again. The girl ripped the hems of the wet outer dresses into strips and retied Buford's leg, then they rode the rest of the day and into the evening draped in satin dresses like blankets.

As dusk settled and the sky glowed hot amber in the wake of the storm, the gable of a two-story house with the roof and walls still intact floated slowly past them, and through the broken glass of the gable window sprawled a pale white lady limp with her arms in the water and blood running down the siding. Her, too, they watched pass in silence.

Still the rain poured, violent drifts of it sometimes blowing backward in the wind to stab into the half-walled shack. Sheets of it flashed before them like ghosts, the long unbroken howl of the wind their unearthly cry, like the hollow-chested soulless Devil himself sucking a long inhalation in readiment to blow out the light of the world.

XXII

Buford and the girl awoke squinting into the bright sunlight, a hot wind billowing the satin dresses from their huddled forms. Buford turned his head from the wind and put a hand to his brow to watch a pair of dresses flying away over a grassy field, the dark fabric silhouetted against the pale blue sky. When the girl shifted against him, he realized his other arm had gone completely dead from her weight. He groaned as she rolled away, the dresses falling from them as she went, and he sat lopsided like a stroke victim, reached across himself and used his good hand to shake his benumbed shoulder and elbow. The broadax fell heavy against the sodden wood floor. He hadn't realized he was still holding it, so lost was his hand. The girl looked at the ax and put her fingers to her lips. Lord God, you could of lopped off my leg in our sleep. She put her toes under the ax handle and scooped it away from them both. Then she gazed around in the sunlight and said, Where in the living world are we?

God only knows, if even Him, Buford said.

The last long wall of the shack was sagging inward, its right hand stud cracked where it joined the floor, bousillage piled on the floor like anthills. Buford winced while he stood, enough use coming into his arm that he could shake it out on its own, and he bent to take up the ax she'd kicked away. With the ax as a crutch to steady himself, he descended carefully from the floor into the wet grass. His right foot was cold and caked in dried blood, and the grass and rainwater that clung to it made a gore over his instep and his toes as he limped his way to the one upright wall to lean on the corner of the shack. To the north and east, wide flat grassland. To the south the same save a shimmering dream of marsh near the horizon, and to the west a thicket of pines and twisted oaks slung with debris tangled in limbs. A pine chair, a pair of wagon wheels, a nest of bedclothes, a broken guitar. A mounted deer head with the antlers intertwined with the branches, the head swinging free as though in a noose they could not see. A child's cane crib and, several trees farther, the child itself.

The girl put a hand to her breast, and Buford lowered his gaze, then collapsed to the edge of the shack floor, his feet splayed so he could massage his right leg. The girl came and sat beside him. You any sense how far we come? she said.

None that I can tell. After a storm such as that, don't know that I could.

The girl looked over at the soggy bundle of mattress and sacks under the leaning wall. You think we'll be able to carry all that back south? You injured as you are?

If we even going south. Near's I could see, we drifted westward from the Calcasieu when it burst, so they's no telling where we ended up. Could be cross the Sabine into Texas by now.

Lordy, the girl said.

My arm here wakes up and my leg ain't rot, I might could climb one them trees and see what I can see. We know more then.

I'm hungry, the girl said.

You'll be hungry a long while yet, sha.

They reposed together for an hour as terns borne in on the stormy winds soared southward overhead and a whir of insects started up in the meadow to their east. Buford, reclined against the upright wall, drifted into sleep, and when he woke again the girl had yanked a sack from inside the mattress and was sorting the goods within it.

What you doing, sha? he said.

I'm looking for what we can leave and what we can carry.

Leave the mattress, then, and use that rope to make us slings for them sacks.

Buford touched his swollen calf and hissed at the pain of it, but hauled himself up anyway and stretched his back. He spied the long pole he'd saved behind the unfurled mattress, and he slid it out and used it as a staff to amble into the trees. The girl averted her eyes as he pissed in the bushes, but then she heard him scrambling upward, grunting or cussing his bad leg, and she turned to watch him until he'd found a steady limb a dozen feet up. Assured he wouldn't fall and die, she bent to the sacks. She set aside in one pile two small cookpots, a pair of tallow candles, a few small knives, a ball of twine. In a second pile she tossed Buford's shattered and bent lantern, his heavy carpentry tools, a fistful of buttons carved from muskrat bones.

Buford had been aloft only two minutes when he called down

to her from the pine. I be damned if I don't recollect that they road.

There's a road? The girl stood from her work at the second sack, a fork and a turtleshell bowl and a folded bit of paper in her fingers, and looked around the leaning wall. She put the paper and fork in the turtleshell and with her free hand shielded her eyes from the sun.

It a kind of a road, or used to be.

It lead southward?

Headed out east, and over west of here's a lake or a river. Hard to tell, swole as it is, but if it a river, I reckon it the Sabine. That road must be the one the Confederate garrison up at Fort Nibletts got started.

Lord God, there's a fort nearby? Soldiers and all?

Maybe, but could be in Yankee hands by now.

I pray it ain't.

I pray it empty, because even if our boys is holding out, I's still in trouble over quitting the war. Buford shifted on his perch in the pine and checked his bearings again in all directions. I has a idea, sha. Just you stay put, leave them sacks a minute.

He began his descent, a storm-twisted branch snapping under his feet and him swinging free a moment while the girl cried out, but he got his grip and found another limb and continued groundward. He dropped the last several feet and hollered as he tumbled, gripping his right leg, and the girl ran to help him up. He leaned on her gasping, but he found his feet and stood one-legged while she brought him the pole.

Lookee here, he said, we far enough from that fort and off the road enough I don't know, but seems worth trying.

Trying what? she said. Buford was hobbling back to the

shack and she followed him.

We already got half a house, or some of one anyways. Woods right here, ain't no one near enough to claim any of it. We could just stay put, sha. Set us up a home right here, plant us some fields. Time comes some soldier or road traveller come in this way, war'll be long enough over we can avoid any questions. Change our names.

He braced the pole against the shack and stepped up onto the warped floor.

We do all right here. Even got us a baby crib ready-made. He pointed into the trees.

She shook her head and tossed her handful of items onto the sack to be sorted later. I don't know, she said, but Buford had stooped to the sack and retrieved the folded paper from inside the bowl. Just leave it, Buford, I'll sort it later. He put the paper in his pocket.

Sha, he said, I mean to make a life with you, and you and me both know Remy's mama ain't gonna let us be in peace. This our chance. We done been delivered by flood like Noah hisself.

You want shut of Mother's meddling more'n you want me, I reckon.

Hell no. You go back in the bayou I will surely follow, difficult though it be on this here leg. I don't know how I could do otherways. I's yourn, from now til Doomsday. Always have been.

Always? What of Remy? Your own true friend, him near a brother to you. You was pining for me even when Remy and me was married?

Since before, sha. He saw you first, the only reason I let you be. Now that ain't a issue, cept Remy's mama keep dragging Remy into things. But he ain't got naught to do with you and me, and she ain't neither. This about me and you, us alone, and I love you.

Hell, Buford.

Not where I's standing.

Remy was my husband. I know I married him half outta desperation, I admit it, but he was a good'n and I tell you true, I loved that man. Your friend. And whatever she might of done between us since you come back, I owe his mama my very life, and more.

She owe you least as much.

I know, but that's the point. We was in it together, and she ain't left me. I can't leave her. I need to go back, least make sure she's alive and if she ain't, help put her in the ground.

Buford put his face in his hands then pushed his fingers through his thick black hair. Damnation, girl. He craned his neck and pointed into the trees beyond, the dead child in the branches. That they petit, you see him? Far's we know Remy's mama in the same position, slung up in some tree north of the marsh, or else washed clear to Lake Charles and drowned. We about as north, it's possible. Ain't no way she floated off safe like we done, that hut of y'all's would never of survived.

We can't assume it, Buford. I know you're right about the hut, but that's just more the reason for going back. If she made it through same as us, she can't rebuild her ownself. Took us work enough to put up even that old straw hut the two of us.

She took Buford's hands in hers. Looked up into his dark face.

You want me, I mean all of me, for now and forever, you need to give me this. Let me go back, make right by her, and then I can leave with no ill conscience to speak of.

Buford looked down at her. Her dark red hair, her black eyes. Her thin lips, her soft sun-browned cheeks under sharp cheekbones. He dropped her hands and put one hand into his hair again and the other into his pocket. She heard the crinkle of the paper in there. He looked off east, then he shook his head and watched over her shoulder as though awaiting some visitor.

She's Remy's mama, Buford. The woman what birthed the man you and I both loved.

Shit, he said. Well, just hell and all. He glanced at her stacks of provisions, those they would carry and those they would leave. He looked back at her. He said, I supposed we oughta just head south to the Gulf and then strike out east from they, so's we don't overshoot our reed beds.

After the girl stripped a supply of bandages from the last of the satin gowns and redressed Buford's leg, they each tied a sack on their backs. Buford leaned on the pole and the girl took up the ax, and they walked the flat earth slowly and with a constant eye to the sun for direction. The grasses were soggy and compacted from the deluge but the way was open. When they encountered trees they were far between, tall pines mostly though some of the younger had bent in the storm and a few lay toppled in their path. Buford climbed the fallen trunks with tremendous care and the girl helped him, and they kept on as best they could.

A vast stretch of boggy marshland only several miles south of them waylaid their already slow progress and by noon had diverted them southwestward. The girl worried at the added distance they were creating, certain that by the time they reached the Gulf they'd have crossed into Texas, though Buford assured her if they reached the Sabine they'd simply follow the bank rather than cross it. Still they trod onward, though even on their new course over somewhat firmer ground, by the time the sun set over a coal-colored horizon they'd only just managed to clear the waist-deep murk and find shelter in a copse of trees.

Along the way they'd found a tall persimmon and collected the bitter fruits not yet ripened. They devoured a few handfuls apiece and afterward lay on the saturated earth with stomachs writhing. Three times each they rolled to their knees and crawled away to the edge of the water to empty their dark fluid bowels. The moonless night passed over them in agony.

Still, in their calmer moments between bouts of diarrhea, they held each other, Buford's wounded leg propped on one of the sacks, and they listened to the songs of insects in the dark. The shrill screech of a distant owl. The ripples in the nearby marsh as reptilian creatures unseen hunted the black.

The second day they crossed a stream then walked as south-ward as they could, but only an hour into their morning they were again disrupted, the meandering waterways of the marshland giving way to a wide brackish lake. They stood awhile on the shore of it judging their direction until, with only the hint of scattered islands to the southeast and the depth of the water unknowable, they determined they had little choice but to round the lake westward.

By midday the lakeshore was behind them and the marsh appeared at times almost solid as a prairie. The sky was near white with sunlight and on the thin brown line of the southern horizon, they spied the smoking hump of a lonesome settlement. They near broke into a run as they aimed for it.

The once-yellow home now faded eggshell and peppered

with wet dust hunkered between a rail fence and large pond green with plant debris blown or washed there in the storm. Three wagons huddled together beside the brown barn and they could hear the braying of mules, the snorts of pigs. A chicken coop nearby. A garden in the rear, the smaller fence disappeared around the back of the house. A gang of five women on the porch in rockers sipping tea or something like it. The middle two among them rose from their chairs as Buford and the girl neared the fence, and one of them said, Lordy, Lordy. The girl climbed the fence without word and the nearest one standing waved her sideways.

Hold on there, girl, there's a gate yonder!

Buford was halfway up the fence himself but he dropped again and limped over to the gap in the fence while the girl ran ahead.

We're sorry, truly we are, but it's a long road and we're just done for. My— She looked back at Buford and watched him hobble up toward the house. My husband's wounded and we ain't had nothing to eat in near two days cept some bad persimmons.

Persimmons? The eldest of the women rolled her head in disbelief. Child, we haven't even had our frost yet, persimmons ain't good to eat for some time yet.

Buford now at the porch answered her. I know it but we was desperate.

Where've y'all come from? the standing woman said.

We just washed in— But Buford interrupted the girl.

Got us lost in the storm, don't quite know where we is. Trying for south, though.

You sound from south, the eldest lady said. She was leaning forward in her chair and squinting at Buford's leg. Your wife said you were wounded?

Buford looked at the girl but spoke to the women. Yes'm, in the war.

Looks fresher than the war, son.

True that, they's some Yankees up Fort Nibletts—

They took that fort clear back in June, son.

I, well sure, ma'am, I know it. Don't mean I like it. Got myself into a bit of a scrape with one.

I hope he fared worse'n you, one of the other women said.

A might worse, ma'am.

Well, we're fair full up here now, the standing woman said. I'm Missus Arnold Stone, name of Catherine, and this is my home. This here's Missus Sarah Hopely and Missus Rose Pryor, both refugees during the war I've let stay on til their husbands return or they get word otherwise. That youngest there is Miss Phoebe Gay, come to visit, and at the end there is Missus Cornelia Yates McGuire. She gestured toward the older woman.

Ma'am, Buford said. Ma'am, ma'am, ma'am, ma'am. The women nodded as he said it. My name's Julius Guidry, and I reckon you met my, um, wife.

Indeed, Catherine Stone said. You said you'd not eaten? Can we offer you a little dinner?

A little dinner'd be fine, ma'am, the girl said.

I hope you don't take offense, Catherine Stone said, but I'll bring the food out here. You may certainly wash in the basin around back, but you do seem to have been through a lot.

No offense indeed, Buford said, and he led the girl around the house until they found a pair of large rain barrels, one uncovered. They unstrapped their sacks and nearly collapsed just from the sudden change in weight, then they each drove their whole torsos headfirst into the barrel. After they'd each dunked again and shaken off what mud and sweat they could, Buford unlidded the second barrel and drove his head in again to drink, and the girl did the same.

Lord God, Buford gasped while the girl was taking her second dunk in the drinking barrel.

When they returned to the porch they found a small table set with two plates of creamed carrots, raw turnips, fried potatoes, and poached eggs, with a bowl of blackberries and a plate of cornbread between the two dinners. Two glasses of milk.

We'd only just ate our own dinner, Catherine Stone said, so you're welcome to it. I wish I could offer you some meat, but we're frugal with our stock here as we're waiting our husbands' return and want to save the feast for them.

Buford only nodded, his mouth already full of the potatoes.

This here's awful nice of you, the girl said. We'd of been happy just for a bit of the cornbread.

A body can't live on cornbread alone, old Cornelia McGuire said, least of all a sick body. That ain't quite what the Good Book says, but it is close enough to truth.

We know what suffering you must have endured, not just on this trip but throughout the war, said the youngest, Phoebe Gay. We are all in this together.

The girl raised a fork and opened her mouth but Buford touched her arm and she stayed herself, though he caught her mutter, You ain't known suffering, in a tone the women couldn't hear.

You make sure'n eat those blackberries, old Cornelia Mc-Guire said. They'll help offset the ailments you must have suffered from those unripe persimmons.

Buford shoved a fistful into his mouth, the dark juice bursting down his thin-bearded chin. Two of the women, he saw not which, said, Oh, my! and giggled as though touring a menagerie.

When they'd got through most of the plates and were dipping their cornbread into their milk, the girl said, I sure appreciate all of this, but y'all didn't have to serve us yourselves. Ain't y'all got any niggers?

We had a few but sold them for food and supplies before the Proclamation came. Seemed a prudent means of securing our investments from Yankee meddling. We knew some with larger holdings than we had who took their slaves with them into Texas. But we never had but a dozen or so anyway, and we've managed well enough for now.

Don't know what we'll do when the men return, Mrs. Rose Pryor said. Can't do the work we used to without our slaves, and I will not allow a freed nigger to work for my husband's money after he fought a whole war just to hold onto them for free. But I don't know a white man worth a penny who'd stoop to nigger's work. I'm sure you would agree, Mister Guidry?

I'd kill, cheat, and rob before I did a nigger's work, Buford said.

Well, I don't know if I'd go that far, but I understand your meaning.

After their dinner, Mrs. Sarah Hopely, wishing to prepare herself for what wounds her husband might bring home, insisted on inspecting Buford's leg, and Charlotte Stone brought out a jar of turpentine. The women all gathered around as though at a medical theater and helped the girl cut loose the satin wraps. Buford's calf was thick, the entry and exit wounds from Whelan's stiletto dark yellow with bright scarlet rings at the edges, the slit of the wound puckered and crusted in blood wet and pale with pus. The women all hissed and cooed, and Rose Pryor all but fainted. But Sarah Hopely scraped and cleaned the wounds with turpentine, Buford wincing but gritting his teeth among the women, then Sarah Hopely soaked two strips of the girl's satin in more turpentine, folded and pressed them one to each wound, and finally wrapped the whole calf with the last of the bandages the girl had ripped from the dresses.

Charlotte Stone offered them the barn for one night and, early though it was, Buford and the girl retired to it, practically bowing backward as they went, as though bidding farewell to royalty. But once in the barn the girl revealed her plans.

We done found us everthing you wanted, Buford, and it just here for the taking.

Girl, we got a long ways yet to walk, what in creation you even talking about?

There's a house with stock and a garden, a pond for fishing I reckon, and them just a group of women to defend it. Between you and me, we could kill them all, in their sleep if we had to but even awake I reckon, and then we'd have the house you wanted far away from Mother.

Sha, you motier foux.

Buford, it's perfect. Once they're dead and buried you can rest here while I carry on south to Mother, get her set up without her never knowing where I'm headed. Then I can leave her free of guilt and come back here to live our lives together.

And what of they men? You heard least two of'm's awaiting

they men from the war.

It's been months now that war was over. How long'd it take you to get back home? If their husbands was coming back they'd be here already.

And the young one still of courting age? You think they ain't menfolk nearby? And that old one, Miss Cornelia? I don't trust that one. She as sly as a old mammie, that'n, probably know her some voodoo or something.

Buford—

War is over, sha. Whelan's dead. Our killing's done.

It'd just be this last time, to make our lives for good. Ain't we earned that?

We earned plenty, sha, that's what I's worried about. This here, after they took us in and fed us, it ain't right. I'll do what you ask, ain't got no choice in it seeing's you bewitched me so, but I's asking you not to ask it. Not this.

They watched each other in the afternoon light, stark bars of sunlight slashing through the barn walls to cut across their faces. She took his hands. She said, How's your leg?

It's a world better, to tell it true. Still smarts when I walk on it, but I could walk a piece yet.

Even now?

What you asking?

I'm asking we leave. If we ain't gonna stay, I'd rather not stay, I'd rather just get on.

They re-sorted their packs but kept most of what they had. Then they scoured the barn for what else they could use, scraps of leather and a few small tools. The girl sneaked out to the coop to gather what eggs she could find while Buford crawled on his belly into the garden to pull up a fistful of carrots, small potatoes, a few squash. They reconvened in the barn and determined their path then they struck out toward the high grasses along the pond, stepped into the water and waded as low as they could without wetting the sacks on their backs, creeping westward to the far edge of the pond and then moving southward. As they left the water they heard a woman calling after them but whose voice it was neither of them could tell.

Buford's leg had improved and with relatively open prairie before them they made good time, walking clear into twilight before giving in to the darkness. They settled in the grasses and the girl gathered scant wood for a small fire over which they boiled and mashed two potatoes and poached an egg apiece. In the distance they saw the faint glow of firelights brighter than their own. They let their fire die out so as not to attract visitors, and they huddled in the dark. The girl fell fast asleep and snored in the night as a thin sliver of the waxing moon emerged, but Buford lay awake for hours just to feel the touch of her hand on his arm.

When they reached the chenier the next day, they found themselves in what once was a road, the flotsam of homes strewn on either side of it. There was smoke a ways up the old road and they followed the thin column til they found a crowd of folk huddled and stunned.

Where we at? Buford asked a woman on the fringes of the huddle.

This here's Johnson Bayou, she said, or used to be.

You lose any? the girl asked.

Lost one. Old Jessop, ain't no sight of him but his boots.

We's sorry to hear it, Buford said.

A shrunken old man put a hand on Buford's shoulder. I don't suppose you could stay a spell and help us gather in what's left some? the old man said. I hate to ask but some of us ain't up to the task.

We can't stay, the girl said, and as she finished saying it they were already following the chenier east.

I understand, the old man called after. Each to his own. They were already out of earshot, his voice being so thin with age, when he added, Godspeed you both straight to Hell.

XXIII

The woman staggered cold and weary through the standing water into Leesburg, most everything she'd known there swept flat. Fragments of furniture indistinguishable from fragments of homes, all splintered boards and rent fabrics for nearly six miles across the town and upriver, most of it from places the townsfolk didn't even know. As she trudged along the main road she saw in each small yard people holding up fractured curiosities and debating their origins.

A pair of men walked into town holding a small boy, wall-eyed and wide-mouthed as though screaming though no sound issued, and continued past the woman to a storm-raked foundation. This here's your home, one of the men said. That's where your bed used to be, I reckon, fore it floated off with you. The boy ran to the spot and curled up in the dirt, arms white around his knees, where he trembled with what would have been sobbing if any tears would fall or cries emerge from his taut throat. The woman watched him a long minute, then turned her head, then walked on.

She went in search of the old boarding house but it was gone. The square of packed earth where it had stood shone paler than the ground surrounding it but otherwise was brushed clean of any trace, the house disintegrated, uncreated as though by the breathy command of God.

In the trees left standing around the town, she found bloated gray corpses slack and sodden hanging from the branches or half-caked in silt and seaweed. She circled the town and counted seven herself; she climbed each tree and plucked loose what jewelry or cash she could, carefully ripping open pockets at their seams. With her pocketknife cutting the fingers off bloated hands to get at the rings. A few people watched her, but those that did said nothing, just trundled on their dazed path through the wreckage.

Three buildings remained mostly standing, walls leaning inward and roofs stripped so the sun shone inside. The survivors had gathered in various locations but most were crowded into the shattered shell of the courthouse. The ripping wind and water had shorn them of their clothes; most wore only scraps and rags or wrapped themselves in rescued blankets, and no one in their bewilderment and grief bothered much with modesty. Everyone present wore some bruise or gash from debris.

The two remaining buildings, one the bank and the other a house that had no business still standing with so many others washed away, were empty, but behind the second she found a man and a woman limp on the ground just beyond the foundation and lashed to an anvil by twenty feet of rope. Sea-thinned blood clung to the woman's slack face in dried rivulets, and the man clung to her with his head buried in her bosom. A ring glinted on the man's finger, but when the woman reached for it he jumped awake and clung tightly to his wife. The woman leapt rearward then backed away. The man was babbling not at her but at the dead woman in his arms. Cheer up, Josephine, he said, his fingers in her bloody hair as he gazed into her dead eyes, shouted at her as though still speaking above the roar of the hurricane. Just you stay with me, my love, it'll all be over soon.

She searched the last of the grounded bodies in ditches or pinned under silt against the foundations of houses, but they had already been pulled loose and looted by some opportunist before her. Later she learned a dozen bodies altogether remained tree-slung or partially interred, and another dozen were missing. Some said they'd watched as friends went bobbing out to sea, clenched and wept as parents or siblings were sucked from their desperate grasp and hauled down into the rushing surf.

Someone had found a calf hiding in a copse of trees and they coaxed it out and led it into the town where the citizens fell upon it with bricks and loose boards, a gang of them bludgeoning the calf about the neck and head until they'd managed to kill it. It took three men the whole afternoon to butcher the calf with just one good skinning knife and a few pocketknives, but they'd got it carved and were roasting hanks of veal over a fire of old furniture in the square, and the woman slipped in among the survivors and took a piece of veal.

A man wandered along the edge of town, on his way out, but with no buildings to conceal him someone in the meat line spotted him and pointed. He carried a basket heavy with provisions and trailed behind him four children like ducklings. He said something to the children and they ran ahead of him as he walked more briskly out of town, but several of those from the meat line gave chase. When they reached him, they surrounded him. They made gestures toward the group around the meat fire, but the man kept shaking his head and clutching his basket tighter against his chest. After several minutes, the posse pushed him off his balance and dragged the basket from his grasp. He struggled to keep hold, but they shoved him into the dirt. A few men and women kicked him to keep him down. The children turned and, seeing their father fallen, ran back and attacked the townsfolk, but all four, small and frail, were flung repeatedly aside like rags. The posse came running back to the fire with fruit and vegetables like a cornucopia aloft in their collective hands, and the meat line tore into the stash and ate the produce uncooked.

When the people had eaten and the sun was dipping in the west, a group gathered to collect the corpses and the woman joined them in case she'd missed a ring, a coin. They carried the bodies out and down to the shore now several yards closer to town. A preacher said a few words over some and a priest performed a brief Mass for the others, and then the townsfolk tossed the bodies into the Gulf to float them out to sea. But the surf, still choppy and swift, brought the bodies back in, and then again. So as dusk settled, they hauled out great sections of the ruined houses, and tables and wagon beds and the cross from the church, and piled it all into a wide bier on the beach. Then they tossed on the corpses and set them ablaze. As it burned, the townspeople sat up in the dunes and watched it solemnly, but the woman slipped away in the dark and began picking her way back into the marsh.

When she arrived at what she thought her patch of earth, she hunted for the remnants of their hut. She found scraps caught in the reeds, some rags and strips of canvas, the heaviest of the iron cookware. She gathered what she could and studied the bald patch for a place to keep it safe, and then she remembered the rain barrel and the hole in the earth. She ran to the spot, no need of a hole or rain barrel to guide her so familiar was the path, and pawed at the deep indentation where the hole used to be. Her fingernails caught on the rusted rim of the buried stovepipe and she clawed into the loam, pulling fistfuls from the pipe. The earth went muddy the deeper she dug, wet as much from the recent flood as from the tears falling heavy but silent from her face. Her teeth gritted, her jaw muscle jumping, her breath frozen in her lungs. But the bottle was gone.

She ripped the stovepipe from the hole, twisted it in her hands then crushed it to her breast. She inhaled in ragged bursts of air, held her breath a moment, then let out a long, quiet moan. She looked at the pipe. She hurled it into the reeds. She stood and screamed toward the Gulf, one long shriek with her fists at her temples, and the wind blew against her. She screamed until she folded in on herself like an accordion to press out the last shaky notes. Then she simply sat in the dirt. Her shoulders quaking but her voice lost to her.

She woke some hours later still curled up on the dirt, the moon a thin blade in the sky. She rolled onto her back and looked at it. Oh, Alphonse, she said. And then she didn't speak again for days.

XXIV

When the girl gathered her rags and borrowed Buford's broadax to return to the woman, Buford protested but she explained again what she felt she owed the old woman. I'll die without you, sha, he said. They huddled in the shade of the small lean-to they'd fashioned from washed-in driftwood and the sewn-together sacks. Somewhere in the vicinity of Buford's former land though they couldn't be sure, even his hearthbricks gone in the hurricane.

But she assured him: I ain't leaving you. I'll just be over there like before for a spell. I'll come back in the night to lay with you and spend my days there to help. Won't take but a week and I'll be back ever night with your supper.

You best. He clutched his chest and lay back on the bed of rotted reeds they'd kicked together on the ground. I can't sleep no more without you, the way I could never sleep proper without a drink but now they ain't no drink to have. You is my drink and the only peaceful nights I have.

Hush, she said. You talk like a fool. Besides, you held onto that whiskey or whatever it is Clovis stills regardless any argument I made, that jug hard in our backs all the long walk home. You really that useless without me, you go on and sup some.

You is hard on a man.

Then get comfortable, cause I don't get no easier.

And then she left him.

She returned through an alien marsh undone and reformed by the storm, but after a few hours walking by sunlight and by feel she found the old site of the hut. Nothing there remained save the bald earth where the hut had stood and the woman herself, squatting over the unearthed firepit and attempting a flame. When the girl arrived she only looked up but made no other sign of recognition.

The girl went and squatted beside her. They sat there for some moments. Finally, the girl spoke.

I come to help you rebuild.

The woman nodded.

I'll stay long as you need me.

It's about damned time.

The woman dug in the pocket of her dress and held out a collection of rings and a pocket watch. The girl regarded them but said nothing.

I found these over in Leesburg. Hell of a sight. I figure I done come by these my ownself and they's mine, but now you come back and offered to help me, I's happy to share'm with you.

What am I gonna do with some old rings?

Ain't nothing to do but sell'm. I was thinking about heading out to old Clovis and swapping for some food. Ain't nothing much left here. The woman looked away toward what once was the back of the hut, the spot where the rain barrel had stood, a divot in the ground washed clean by the storm surge. She sighed and shook her head. But I'd be happy to share it with you.

What you eating tonight?

I told you, I ain't got nothing but some old onions and a couple oranges. You welcome to them already if you get this here site started, set us a tent while I run out to Clovis and try and get us some food.

Tonight?

Right now. If'n you don't mind.

I'll help you, but I don't know. Tonight? You sure you'll be all right?

I'll be better out they than stuck here trying to rebuild. They's a reason I ain't started yet. This here's young folk's work. Leave the walking to me.

It's a late start, though, probably be dark before you get back.

The woman jingled the rings and replaced them in her pocket. It a light enough load and I don't plan to fool with Clovis all day. Besides, I reckon it don't get much darker than it already got, storm like we come through. She stood with a groan and rubbed her knee then stretched her back. You go on and eat you a supper of what's left and get you to bed early. I'll be back fore you fall asleep.

And without further word the woman hiked off to disappear in the reed beds.

The girl looked around the camp for a moment, saw a few weary goods: sacks unstitched and flattened in the dirt, some cane poles and reeds the woman had pulled up and piled. The girl found a clay bowl full of water and she bent and checked her reflection. Buford would not understand and she knew it. She'd have to explain that she meant to stay til the work was through, that she wouldn't return tonight. She hurried to get the tent set up and the dinner cooked before sunset so she could run back through the reeds to tell him by dark.

The woman never went near Clovis's lakeside store. Instead, she hiked directly north into the lowlands to find the tree where she'd tied her sack. The ground was soft and muddy still, a few inches of silky silt resting in the shallows, the trees flocked with mud several feet high on their trunks. It took her the rest of the afternoon to hunt out the tree she was looking for, but finally she found it, her package hanging by loosened ropes from the tree branch but the knots about the sack itself still fixed. She shimmied up the tree and out on the top branch, loosened the ropes until the sack fell and she caught it in an arc out of the air then lowered it by the ropes and climbed down again.

She undid the knots and opened the sack to find her stash inside soaked but intact. The hide was patchy and reeked of swamprot. The fur on the mask was matted and filthy, the leathery lips shrunken away from the teeth and the bone of the muzzle showing near the face, which made the terror of it all the worse. She grinned when she saw it. Then she closed the flap of the sack and hiked back to stash it in the marsh.

The sunset burned red on a smoky horizon behind her as the girl rushed off through the reeds to see Buford, partly to explain that she would be staying with the woman for a while and partly because she missed him. The air was hot and she was soon slick in sweat but she ran on anyway, panting but eager to be there and back before the old woman returned, just to avoid the explanation. The going was awkward in the newly unfamiliar terrain. In the faint breeze a reek of dead rodents and wet dog and rotting plant life stronger than she'd imagined would still remain. And darkness settled sooner than she'd expected it. But there was light left enough for her to see looming up out of the shadows the lurking shape of the rougarou, patchy and reeking of the swamp and seeming to drool in the shadows.

She threw out her hands and slid wildly to nearly fall in the thin mud and she screamed. Turned to flee back into the marsh, the crash of the rougarou behind her.

She slipped and wheeled her arms and fell once to her knees but scurried on. The wash of burgundy sky hot ahead of her and filling her with dread.

She could hear the rougarou on a parallel course with hers, pounding through the reeds and grunting as it came. She twisted and zagged south to hide in the thicker parts of the marsh, there to lose it. After a while the pursuit seemed to ebb and though she ran still, her dress soaked in sweat and the hem heavy with dark silt, she turned northwest again and sought frantically to find her way back to the site of the old hut, near lost in the storm-altered terrain.

It was full dark by the time she burst into the old woman's makeshift tent and there she folded up and hid herself in a ball in the back corner.

Later, deep night now and a slice of moon like a scythe low over the horizon, the woman returned to find the girl cringing in the dark.

Hey, she said, toeing the girl. The girl flinched in the dark. Why ain't you got us a fire going? I could hardly make my way back in the dark.

The girl made no reply.

What the matter with you? You sick? The woman bent and flung back the blanket but the girl cried and dragged it back, though she left her face uncovered now.

Lord, the woman said. You sure look pale, like to glow in the dark, face like the moon. It ain't natural.

The girl looked up through the tops of her eyes at the woman and her voice came small but determined.

It ain't nothing.

In his lean-to, Buford sat getting drunk on the whiskey, and he waited for the girl but she never came. He sucked at some hard-tack then downed the last of his drink and limped out into the reed beds where he stood muttering to himself: Where she at? Damn fool, she done run off with that old witch. I do miss her teats. I knew they'd light out on me, leave me here to rot. Old witch. Foul old witch bitch. He reared back and hollered into the reeds: Old bitch!

As if in answer, a long howl floated over the reeds and Buford stood with his head cocked. He shouted again. Bitch! For a moment the marsh admitted no sound at all, every living thing gone silent, but then he heard the howl again and it sounded closer. He stepped backward toward his lean-to until he tripped and fell into it, his legs in the air. He rolled onto his side, added wood to his fire until it glowed bright yellow and too hot on his face, and he crawled deep into the angle of his lean-to where he huddled shivering and weeping in silence until he passed out.

The morning broke hot and humid, with thick white clouds hanging over the Gulf. The woman and girl erected heavy poles in their clearing for a new hut. Between shaping the pole-ends with Buford's ax and driving the stakes into the earth, their stomachs rolled and growled with hunger. Finally the girl rested her weight on a stake and asked the old woman why she didn't bring back any food from Clovis.

I'd of liked to, but Clovis ain't got nothing left to trade, done been flooded out in the hurricane.

The girl shook her head and resumed jabbing fiercely at the earth, driving a pole into the ground, her face a mask of angry determination. Then her twisted features collapsed into wonderment and then drew back, her eyebrows high as she thought of something, and she looked at the woman.

What you think happened to all them bodies we put down the well?

The woman smiled at her grimly.

I reckon they flooded out and floated off somewheres. Ain't nothing for us to worry about now. After that storm, they's none'd think we had nothing to do with'm.

I was thinking about that last one. That old lieutenant.

The rougarou?

He weren't no rougarou, just a man in a old mask.

I told you he might look thataways but he's more'n a man now. Devil owns your soul, he don't let you off so easy.

So you're saying he might of somehow crawled up out that

hole to keep after Buford?

I's saying crawled up or washed up, he out now either way, and the Devil what owns him got more important things on his mind than war deserters and Jayhawkers. Why? You seen him?

I ain't seen nothing.

You best walk careful out on the marsh these nights just the same. We both best.

The girl stabbed again at the earth and they set to another stake. She agreed to stay with the woman again that night, but as the sun set she stood in the flap of the tent gazing wistfully out over the reeds. The fire flared up in its pit and the woman sat beside it boiling a thin soup of grasses and wild onions. She called to the girl.

Hey, you gonna stare at the marsh or you gonna come get you some supper?

I ain't seen Buford in two days now. I'd of thought he'd of come to see me.

I told you he only interested in the one thing, and now he too lazy even to chase it. Expects you to bring it to him.

That ain't fair.

He ain't here, is he?

He's wounded. Or maybe he seen...

Seen what? You was lying before, you did see you a rougarou, didn't you?

I don't know what I saw.

You saw something, though.

I just need to know he's all right.

Buford takes fine care of hisself, I need you here. You want to see him you go in the daylight.

I didn't think you'd let me. Not without no fight, anyways.

Well they I agree with you.

But you're right about the timing of it. Only it's too late in the daytime now to try it. But just so we ain't got no argument, I'm saying it now. In the morning I'm going to see him.

Well, if the Devil tempts you, I suppose it only right you tempt him back.

Buford ventured into the reeds at night hoping to sneak in on the girl and whisk her away, but out in the night he encountered the shape of the rougarou. He froze in the marsh and watched it stalk the reeds in the dark, the resurrected wolf unkillable, and he grew scared because he wondered now how many were after him, or if the old woman might have been right. There was plenty a person could get up to, he reckoned, and maybe that lieutenant had a voo-doo spell cast over him somehow.

During the day, Buford lingered in the reeds near the emerging hut, but seeing the girl there cooperating with the woman, he grew angry and he left her there, retreated into the reed beds and back to his site to rebuild his house, for her or without her, either way.

Without his tools, he hiked out to Clovis's to strike a trade. The old boardwalk was gone, ripped away in the storm, but the foundation piles the shop stood on were driven deep and fixed firm to the foundation, and though it leaned dangerously, the store remained. Buford swam out to the broken steps and climbed up to the porch and pushed inside. The shack reeked to bring bile to Buford's throat and he could see even in the dim light it was aban-doned. He stood in the doorway and searched the gloom until he found Clovis's waterlogged corpse stuck up in the rafters with his neck ripped open and a pair of crawfish living inside the wound. Beside him in the rafters sprawled the black gimp, drowned so he looked asleep, and at first Buford didn't recognize him. In peace he looked more adult than Buford remembered, death relieving him at last from the head wound that had so long suppressed him, and Buford realized for the first time how big he was. The whore Marceline was nowhere.

Buford studied the corpse of Clovis, the gaping wound in his neck not sliced open but rent with great ferocity, and he thought of the rougarou, and he ran from the shack so fast he fell in the lake where the boardwalk had once been. He thrashed in the water until he got his feet and he began to swim hard away but he stopped, treaded water to think. He turned and waded back, crept back into the shack, and set to digging through debris and collecting what few rusty tools he could. Two saws and a hammer and a hatchet. Then he jumped back in the lake and returned to his own lonely homestead.

In the morning, the women picked at the last of the soup and an orange.

Ain't we got more to eat than this?

I done told you, the woman said, old Clovis ain't got nothing left to sell.

Well maybe he's got something by now. Maybe we ought to go see together.

It too dangerous in the dark or the light of day and you know it. You know what you saw. We'll just eke on as we always done.

We ain't got nothing to make do on.

Well we can't both go. It too hot to go by day and I done been there in the dark once myself, I suppose I can risk it again.

The girl thought to protest again but saw her chance and agreed with the woman. Rougarou or no.

That night the woman left as dusk settled. The girl waited until she was sure it would be safe, then she took a knife and, hearing the call of the rushes, she ran out into the reed beds for Buford's, this time taking a different path.

But in the reeds she encountered the rougarou again, smelling it before she saw it. She ran in wild arcs trying to get around the decaying wolf, but it stayed with her and in the end she fled back to the hut, calling Buford's name.

To mask her cries the wolf began to howl.

In the distance, Buford heard the howling and grabbed his hatchet and ran into the reeds but only got a few paces before he thought it safer to retreat and remain near the light of his fire.

And in the darkness the woman waited until she was sure, and she lifted off the fetid mask and grinned into the night. She turned the mask to face her, stroked its pelt and rubbed one ear.

I be damned but I begin to comprehend you after all.

XXV

At the woman's tent the girl began having dark dreams. She imagined Buford creeping up on the tent and when he opened his mouth to call her name she only heard a howl. His jaw would rip forward, the bones cracking and muscles tearing in bloody strings, and then his face turned itself inside-out and from the jellied gore emerged the face of the wolf. When she woke upright screaming, Buford really was outside their tent and he ran away. Inside, the old woman watched her.

What the matter, girl? You having dreams?

The girl panted and gasped, one hand on her heart and the other mopping at her brow. She looked at the woman but said nothing.

Might mean something, you know, the woman said. My grandmere was Chitimacha Indian and had a gift with dreams but I never learned it. We could find us a old voodoo nigger to tell us what you saw, though.

But the girl only panted and looked about the tent.

Well, you woke me up and I's only just laid down.

The old woman rose to piss in the reeds and she watched the beds with her nose in the air like a dog. In the distance she could hear a man shouting, something threatening, but she left him be.

In his great frustration Buford raced through the reeds and tore at his shack boards, ripping apart the scattered timbers. He splintered planks lengthwise and flung them wheeling into the reeds. He lifted a long timber over his head and hacked at the ground til it cracked, a gouge in the earth. He grabbed a pair of boards and kicked at them. An exposed nail punctured his foot and he screamed into the night, fell over and passed out on the ground bent fetal with his foot in his hands. When he woke, his foot was still in his grasp, swollen and angry claret flesh with the nail-hole puckered and oozing.

The girl walked down to the pond to fetch water and found Buford huddled there in the reeds. He hissed at her.

Hey. Hey salope. Where you been? You ain't been to see me.

The girl just looked at him, then looked back up the path toward the campsite.

You done growed tired of me? Done had your fill of old Buford, content to leave me stiff like a dead man back they at home?

We ain't neither of us got no home no more.

Buford made to reply but the old woman came down the path and when he heard her approach he ducked into the weeds. The girl rolled her eyes. The two women passed each other, the girl returning to the camp and the woman stepping out onto the planks by the water. She raised her skirt and squatted to piss and with her head low she spied Buford in the reeds. He was watching up the path after the girl, and when he looked back the woman drifted her eyes so as not to appear to have seen him. In this way they regarded each other, Buford shifting his weight off his bad foot and the woman pissing before him. When she finished her piss she looked directly at him and his eyes flew wide. She grinned at him and rose and walked off.

Before dawn the woman kicked the girl awake and handed her a dress patched from scraps of cloth. They sat together on a long log by the fire and checked knots on a collection of stone bolas they'd been making the day before. The reeds danced and the marsh birds stirred in the beds. The girl and woman crept out to find a nest of ducks in the marsh. They found the blind they'd built and sat in it watching the ducks rise with the sun. They sorted and untangled their bolas, pointed in silence to the clusters of birds they claimed, and then rose, one at a time, to spin each bola tight overhead and hurl it into the knot of ducks. With each throw explosions of birds burst from the marsh, and they counted seconds between their throws, one mississippi two mississippi, to let the ducks settle again. But before they'd loosed half a dozen bolas the ducks had all moved on to safer grounds, and the women waded out to retrieve the dead ones. As they returned to the campsite the girl separated out one of the ducks and handed the rest to the woman.

I'm gonna take this'n on over to Buford, he bound to be hungry.

You can't go off and leave me, we got work to do.

I'll just be gone long enough to give him this and then I'll be back.

You will not, he'll keep you.

Now Mother, we done talked about this. I agree with you about the dangers of night but it's daytime now and I've had enough of not knowing how he is.

Oh go on, then, you gonna do whatever takes your mind anyways.

I am for true. She broke away and the old woman didn't move. The girl said, I'll be right back, before supper I promise. The old woman didn't say anything, just watched her.

As soon as the girl was around a bend in the path and hidden in the reeds the woman sprinted with the ducks back to the campsite and slung them into the tent without stopping. Then she ran back through the reed beds to find her wild wardrobe stowed out in the marsh.

At the lean-to the sky glowed silver over the distant wall of clouds, and when the girl first approached, Buford didn't stand up, he only watched her, the duck swinging at her side. She tossed it at him.

I brung you some dinner.

I don't need nothing.

Horseshit. You a stick, ain't nothing left to you.

That why you don't come round no more? Don't care for how I look?

Damn it, Buford, I can only argue with one ignorant person at a time. I done told you where I'm at and why I'm there. Now take the duck and get to plucking. You want I'll fix it for you before I go.

Buford stood and winced and limped toward the duck. She looked at his swollen foot wrapped in rags, the toes purple.

Lord God, Buford, what'd you do to your foot?

It ain't nothing. I told you I's laid up, but I's laid up before I ever done this. You done flattened me, sha, and I just don't know what to do anymore without you here.

The girl shook her head, said, Oh Buford. She slung her arms around his neck and kissed him, then lifted his arm onto her shoulder and helped him limp to a toppled bucket near the firepit. She sat him down and unwrapped the foot to look at it. He had a deep hole crusted with blood and pus, and in the swollen flesh she could make out a deep red streak winding from the puncture along the instep up onto the bridge of his foot and from there around the ankle to disappear in the hairs on his calf. She turned his foot and pressed on it and he hissed and put a hand on her shoulder.

All them times getting shot at or worse, friends of mine losing arms and legs. We ever run out of guns, we could of fought on in the war using just sawed-off human legs as clubs, many of'm as we compiled by the end. Probably would of won if we had. And I got out all in one piece, hardly a scratch or a scar on me, and here I go about to lose my damned foot.

Hush now.

But they both hushed as a low growl rolled in from the marsh and ascended into a high yowl. They scanned the yard and saw in the distance the shuffling figure of the rougarou, practically on all fours as it crept toward the camp, and the girl shrieked and rose. Run Buford! Buford stood but only hopped on one foot toward his lean-to where he'd laid his knife. The girl watched him hopping and, realizing what he aimed to do, she hissed at him, Buford, you hop off that direction and hide, I'm gonna lead the wolf away.

What the hell you talking about?

She shoved him into the lean-to and she bent to whisper.

It wants me now much as you, and you can't run. I'll lead it off, you just hide.

And before he could protest she had bolted into the reeds straight for the rougarou. He called after her but she ran on. The wolf weaved to meet her coming but she feinted and at the last minute tore off to the north, and sure enough the rougarou ran after.

They ran and ran, north then west then north and sharp east again, avoiding the water and running winding paths over the earth for greater speed. The girl's hair whipping into her face every time she looked back to judge her distance from the rougarou, which was slight and getting smaller. She ran the harder and zagged more erratically, and in the wreckage left from the hurricane the girl misjudged her path and ran straight into the old well.

She didn't even scream.

The woman in costume came crashing into the old homestead after her but, finding the girl missing, guessed what must have happened. She rushed to the now-stoneless lip of the well and peered into the fading light and heard the girl thrashing in there. The woman ripped off the mask and called to her: Hold on, just keep you aswimming, I'll go for rope.

She pitched the mask as she ran and it settled into the mud near the lip. She ran back to her stash in the marsh and tore apart the bundle for the rope that had tied it. She got lost once on her return, ran a quick circle in the reeds until she found her way to the hole, but by the time she returned, the thrashing had ceased. She lowered the rope anyway, called into the hole that echoed wetly back at her. She lay there on the earth dipping and dipping the rope into the water, calling, sobbing, to no avail. In the grass and reeds surrounding her she could see the putrid corpses, some half-decayed, some half-eaten, that had washed up out of the well in the flood. Exactly as she'd described. In the distance she heard a wolf cry but she paid it no attention, and when the reeds stirred nearby and a gator sauntered into the clearing she ignored it too. She kept on dipping the rope.

Buford returned to his lean-to, having gone limping after the girl but losing her, and found a fire going. He limped toward it, scanned about but saw nothing. He whispered into the brush: Hey sha? Hey girl, where you at?

Instead of the girl, he heard a different voice, almost a hiss in the reeds.

Ain't no sha here.

Buford whirled but was caught up by an aimed pistol. He faced a rougarou, smaller and less foul than the one he knew. He peered at it in the firelight. Then he smirked.

You ain't Lieutenant Whelan.

I ain't Whelan but I am a Rougarou, same as him. What one of us wants we all want. You a man of the earth as you are, you ought to have known we hunt in packs. And now I come to finish you.

You go on and get out of here. I ain't afraid of you.

That's good. Dead man shouldn't have no fears. Makes his passing easier.

You just go on to Hell.

I'll get there according to my own time, Buford.

The rougarou lowered the muzzle but then he pulled the trigger, shot Buford in his good foot. Buford fell howling, cried and cussed, held his newly wounded foot just as days before he'd held the other. When the rougarou approached, Buford spit at him.

The rougarou holstered his pistol and leaned over Buford.

Buford lunged from the ground and clawed at the man's throat, clawed at his mask. The rougarou put his thin hands around Buford's neck and pressed down, and Buford swung and punched the mask askew, grabbed the muzzle and ripped the mask loose. The face underneath was cold, featureless as stone, the lips pressed thin and the skin pale against the shock of pale blonde hair gone white in the firelight. He pinned Buford down with one hand and leaned into him, Buford kicking on the ground, and he reached back and took out a long knife. Buford spat in his face.

You do know how to fight, Buford. Shame you didn't use it to the ends you were meant for.

You can fuck youself. Now go on and kill me, God damn you.

The rougarou smiled.

That's rather brave of you, son. You might redeem yourself yet.

He pressed the blade against Buford's throat and Buford stretched his own neck, breathed hard through his nostrils, and the rougarou opened Buford's throat so the blood shot hot and thick, first in one great burst and then in sharp pulses over the rougarou's face, his arms. He did not move, just held Buford down as he died.

In the morning the woman, still dragging the rope, returned

to Buford's clearing where she found his body. A tripod of housing timbers nailed together and driven into the ground, and Buford nailed through his ruined feet, upside-down onto the tallest post with his arms hanging loose several feet above the ground, his head tied back against the post with a coil of twine, blood all down his face and his neck gaping like a second mouth. She sat and stared up at him for a long time, the sun rising behind him.

At noon she woke, unaware that she'd fallen asleep, and she picked herself up from the ground and looked around the clearing. Then she trudged back through the reed beds in an aimless path. Traps and buckets and a boot and dead fish and lost crabs cast up out of the bayou and abandoned by the storm. In a deep wallow of mud the drying corpse of a porpoise. The trees all leaved with grackles. Snakes rippling the puddles. Then her home. The frame of the new hut completed, a skeleton in the yard. The woman looked around, turning the rope in her fists. She put her hand over her eyes and peered squinting up at the sun. Then she bent into the tent, found a long knife, and went into the beds to cut reeds for her roof.

Acknowledgments

Because this book is rooted in both myth and history, it required a great deal of research, which I couldn't have done without the generous help of countless librarians. I especially want to thank the staff at Cameron Parish Library and Calcasieu Parish Public Library. I also found invaluable information at the Acadian Village and Vermilionville Historic Village, both in Lafayette, Louisiana.

I was able to visit these sites and finish my research and drafting of *Hagridden* thanks to the generous support of Literary Arts, who granted me a 2013 Oregon Literary Fellowship.

Many thanks to my agent, John Sibley Williams, and to my publisher, Brad Pauquette, for believing in this book at least as much as I did. And to the literary magazines *Sententia* and *SOL: English Writing in Mexico*, which published early excerpts of *Hagridden*.

I owe a great many other people my gratitude for their support, feedback, and advice throughout my writing career, more than I can name here. But I want to offer special thanks to all my writing teachers: Billie C. Hoffmann, Dani Vollmer, Kathleen Hudson, David Breeden, Jerry Bradley, Robert Flynn, Barbara

Rodman, John Tait, and, through his friendship and advice, Tom Franklin.

I'm also indebted to my family, for their love and support on this long journey to my first novel. Special recognition goes to my late maternal grandmother, Beth Locke, whose letters about life in Louisiana informed many passages of this book.

And, most of all, thanks to my wife and best friend, Jennifer. Her motivation and support got this book started; her belief in the book helped me finish it and led to my fellowship; and her keen critical eye and her skills as a librarian helped make the early drafts of this novel so strong, as she makes me strong.

About the Author
Samuel Snoek-Brown

Samuel Snoek-Brown grew up in Texas and often visited relatives in southwest Louisiana, the region where this novel is set. *Hagridden* is the novel for which he received a 2013 Oregon Literary Fellowship. He is also the author of the fiction chapbook *Box Cutters*, and his work has appeared in dozens of print and online literary magazines. Samuel has a doctorate in creative writing from the University of North Texas and teaches writing and literature in Portland, Oregon, where he lives with his librarian wife and their two cats.

CPSIA information can be obtained at www.ICGtesting.com
Printed in the USA
LVOW11s2144041015

456896LV00002B/70/P

9 780989 173797